Aravind Jayan is from Trivandrum, Kerala. He
of the 2017 Toto Award for Fiction and was shor
Commonwealth Short Story Prize in 2021. He lives

Praise for *Teen Couple Have Fun Outdo*

'When I read his novel last summer, my first thought was: '
Narayan and Roth had a baby", by which I meant it had R.K.
natural lightness of touch, but was not quite as coy. There was a healthy
dose of steaminess and raunch – a sex, lies and videotape vibe. Jayan
looks at his material squarely, yet retains a fleet-footedness' Aatish
Taseer, Books of the Year, *Open Magazine*

'An insouciantly told tale of how a compromising viral video throws a
family into disarray' Books of the Year, Sanjay Sipahimalani, *Wire*

'Witty, hard-hitting and a must read – it could happen to anyone!' Books
of the Year, Rupa Gulab, *Deccan Chronicle*

'Truly infectious ... slicing through inherited ideas around shame,
honour and reputation' *Guardian*

'Told with dry and restrained humour ... *Teen Couple Have Fun Outdoors*
stands out not for what it tackles ... but for its graceful sidestepping of
the usual narrative routes, without any loss of impact or verisimilitude.
Jayan's book is the calling card of a novelist of promise and surprising
maturity' *Times Literary Supplement*

'A breezy tale of intergenerational conflict, with a side order of class
consciousness' *Financial Times*

'Perhaps one of the most original stories to have been published in India
in a long time ... Jayan's craft makes you read the entire book in a single
sitting, almost as if you've just discovered a scandalous report while
scrolling through your phone and just cannot help yourself from being
sucked into every minute detail described' *Mint Lounge*

'This novel about a young couple's sex scandal is an assured debut. With whip-smart humour and pointed observations, Jayan explores the frustrating consequences of the generation gap between parents and children' *Scroll.in*

'A clever, bittersweet book with wit and perceptiveness ... a writer to watch out for' *The Hindu*

'Genuinely funny ... a strong debut novel from a sophisticated new author' *Debut Digest*

'So original, fresh and compelling' *Deccan Herald*

'A brilliant debut novel that will get you begging for more from Aravind Jayan' *Asian Age*

'One of the wittiest, cleverest, most perceptive books I've read about India in years. An acidic comedy of manners, an anarchic demolition of modern Indian mores, as well as a melancholic, sweet-sour love story about the impossibility of being young' Rahul Raina, author of *How to Kidnap the Rich*

'In the age of the internet, still stories of family remain ageless. Jayan sets us in a moment when the past and present are in precarious balance and leaves us to settle for ourselves what has been broken and what will never be. Loved it' Karen Joy Fowler, author of *We Are All Completely Beside Ourselves*

'Humorous, insightful and enormously touching ... an exquisite debut' Clare Allan, author of *Poppy Shakespeare*

'So here it is, at last: an insider view of the clash between generations seen from the perspective of the online Indian Gen Z. Written with wryness, compassion, intelligence, crystal clarity and a dry sense of humour, Aravind Jayan's unputdownable debut features one of the most engaging and Nabokovianly complicated narrators I've encountered in the last God knows how many years. It's impossible not to love this book. You'll laugh and laugh until you find yourself devastated by the last thirty or so pages, and you'll still be laughing. Oh, did I also mention unputdownable?' Neel Mukherjee, author of *The Lives of Others*

Teen Couple
Have
Fun Outdoors

ARAVIND JAYAN

This paperback edition first published in 2023

First published in Great Britain in 2022 by
SERPENT'S TAIL
an imprint of Profile Books Ltd
29 Cloth Fair
London EC1A 7JQ
www.serpentstail.com

10 9 8 7 6 5 4 3 2 1

Typeset in FreightText by MacGuru Ltd
Designed by Nicky Barneby @ Barneby Ltd

Printed and bound in Great Britain by CPI Group (UK) Ltd, Croydon CRO 4YY

A CIP catalogue record for this book is available from the British Library.

ISBN 978 1 78816 987 5
eISBN 978 1 78283 953 8

Teen Couple Have Fun Outdoors

I

Annie Believes in Aliens

1

I knew something was wrong when Sreenath wouldn't come down to see the new car. He said he had a headache, but when I stood outside his room I could hear him talking to someone on the phone. After a few more tries, I let it be.

The car we'd all decided on was a white Honda Civic. It was slicked back for speed and beeped if you didn't wear a seat belt. Appa and I had gone to the showroom earlier that morning. He had driven the car home carefully, avoiding potholes, clenching his body every time he touched the brakes. Halfway through, he'd switched on the GPS and turned up the volume. He wanted to hear the car talk. When he parked in front of our house, he looked only at the Assist screen on the dashboard, no mirrors. If there was a way to deploy the airbags without crashing, he would have done that too.

It was sometime between ten thirty and eleven on a Saturday morning in March. One or two neighbours stopped by to congratulate us. Karthika aunty, our neighbour on the left, told us that her husband was planning to get a Civic as well, but a different model. Why a different model? God only knew. But she was always saying things that made us question what we did. In any case, we were accepting comments and compliments with a certain degree of nervousness. As a financial decision, the car was slightly frivolous. Our previous one, a Maruti Alto, had been doing fine except for the usual problems that came with old age. It would have run for another five years, maybe more with good care. Amma, especially, had been sad to sell it off. She was a certifiable hoarder.

Still, despite all this nervousness, we tried to be pleasant. On the windscreen, Appa pasted the sticker mandated by our housing colony, making sure it wasn't lopsided. We lived in a place called Blue Hills. Blue Hills had around twenty-five houses and I suppose it was situated on a mild incline. The houses looked like the ones you got in Monopoly: seemingly placed there whole. Each one had a car porch and a garden that could hold six or seven potted plants. There was a small park in the middle of the colony where parties were held and children played. For a while in high school, I was considered the official Blue Hills babysitter. I used to spend a lot of time in that park, walking around and listening to music. Parents would come to me and say, 'If you're here anyway, can you do me a favour?' While they were gone, I had to make sure their kids didn't eat sand or throw themselves in front of a vehicle. Thankfully, nobody died on my watch and most of the sand is still there even today. Of all the people who lived with us in the colony, I liked those kids the most.

'Maybe we should have picked silver,' Appa said.

'White is good,' Amma said. 'It's clean. It's tidy.'

After another round of inspection, we went inside for tea and retired to our separate corners.

Sreenath skipped lunch, still claiming a headache, and didn't come down till later that afternoon. While he did show excitement about the car, I could tell he was faking it. Had he been truly excited, he would have started an argument with Appa about his decision to leave the seat plastic on, or scolded me for letting Amma put turmeric streaks on the bonnet. He'd have proffered some advice and made a final ruling regarding the efficacy of our purchase.

Instead, he walked around the car thrice, opened the door, and sat inside for a long time – first with Appa, as he recited the specs, and then alone. After that, he went back upstairs to his room and closed the door.

I next saw him at dinner. Weekends were the only time we all ate together. Sreenath sat down halfway through the meal. Once again, he was quiet and distracted.

'How's the food?' Appa asked him. He was the one who'd cooked that day, as he sometimes did on the Saturdays he was free. That night he'd made prawn curry and rice.

'It's fine,' Sreenath said.

'You don't like it?'

'I told you it's fine. Let me be.'

This had the potential to keep going, so I said something about my internship and switched on the TV.

The rest of dinner was uneventful except for the time the landline rang. Sreenath turned around so quickly, he almost knocked down the water jug. He didn't start eating again until Appa said it was his brother, calling after seeing the car pictures he had sent.

I wasn't the only one who noticed Sreenath's reaction. Amma pestered him non-stop, asking him what was wrong until he shovelled down his food and fled upstairs.

Appa was still going on about the car, now annoyed. 'No no, it's not the kind of white that attracts dust,' he was saying. 'This is *Enamel* White. *Enamel. Enamel.* They use this coating on space shuttles and rockets.' I don't know where he pulled that last fact from, but he seemed pleased.

Afterwards, I heard Amma telling him that Sreenath looked feverish. This was something she often did. Amma tried to diagnose a fever whenever anyone in the house went through some form of turmoil that was unreachable to her. A fever diagnosis put her in control. She'd take our temperature, offer us paracetamol, and tell us to have a nap.

2

Sreenath was twenty-two and I was twenty. Growing up, I was always eager to please him, maybe because he made it seem like he'd toured the world shortly before I was born.

He said things like, 'Honestly, it's better for everyone if Appa and Amma just went their separate ways. Amma can still get someone else to marry her. Appa can maybe keep birds.'

Or, 'The blue liquid in those ads, that's actually blood, you moron.'

Compared to me, he had a lot to say.

The two of us had gone to an all-boys' school run by Jesuits. Sreenath was popular. He acted bored and cynical, most of the cynicism lifted from Appa's tirades about life. I think he peaked when he ran as a joke candidate for school leader. He even did a speech. Though afterwards, people kept telling him 'good attempt', and he had to keep saying, 'Wait, that wasn't a real attempt, the whole thing was a stunt. Did you guys not get that?' Naturally, I benefited from being related to him. Seniors were nice to me and I was always being greeted by people I didn't know.

Academically, too, I suspected that Sreenath was a few watts brighter than me. He would only start studying the night before the exams, all the while complaining about a childhood denied to him by never-ending tests. He would still come out doing well. I, on the other hand, needed coffee on tap, almonds, perfect silence and weeks of moping around to get things done. The only subjects I topped or came close to topping were computer science and Malayalam, and, depending on my teacher's state of affairs with her husband, history. That man cost me a lot of marks.

But maybe this sort of description makes Sreenath seem oversmart and precocious. All said and done, both of us were simply average, him one or two pegs higher, that's all.

The only place I really trumped him was sports. I played as a forward for the school football team and a local youth club. Football used to be my chief excuse to get away from the house. Sreenath was not only worse than me, but the way he played was objectively mangled. Once, he hit an own goal, twisted his ankle *and* tore his shorts in a single go. After that he tried to spin it off like expending energy on sports was a lavish thing, the same as eating too much.

At the time we bought the new car, Sreenath was two years out of university. He was studying to be a chartered accountant while doing his articleship at a local firm. My university had just ended – not the same one as Sreenath's – and I was interning at an English-language newspaper. By then, we were up to different things and hung out in completely separate circles. Mine was a semi-circle, really. Sreenath's was still big, even if diminished by time.

Not many young people stayed in Trivandrum after they graduated. It was a hometown. You couldn't squeeze a lot out of it besides the beach, a few awkward bars, and half a mall. The roads cleaned out by eleven and if you wandered around late, you were likely to get stopped by the police. I'd once read a tourist guide that called the city 'quaint'. It was so quaint that when you woke up on Sunday evenings after a heavy lunch, there was nothing left to do but kill yourself.

Sometimes Amma would be conducting her tuition classes downstairs – she held maths and physics classes twice a week for middle-schoolers – and something about the classroom sounds intensified this feeling of being trapped.

There were still aspects of the city I liked, though. People seemed to have the time to care about the small things, which, when applied in a positive direction, wasn't too bad. The public library, an old building packed with cool air, was something I could never get enough of. The days were soft. You could watch the trees and walk the beach. At the very least, it was comfortable.

That said, the reason Sreenath and I stayed was mostly because Appa had made us stay. He ran a chain of textile shops – Royal Textiles, it was called – and though by that point we had stopped helping out like we used to in school, he'd insisted on having us close by. To validate this, he made us go there once in a while to manage the stocks, clean, or hand out flyers. 'At least for some time.' That's what he said when my university ended. He'd said the same thing to Sreenath. Both of us had somehow agreed. In Sreenath's case, he also had his chartered accountancy course to finish.

Anyway, all this was to say that my brother and I weren't like twins who could read each other's minds. We liked to have our own space. That's why I didn't get after him like Amma did. It could have been the reason he didn't confide in me. Though, that could also have been because he hoped no one at home would find out after all.

Even so, I couldn't help but keep an eye on him. That Monday, Sreenath stayed home on the strength of Amma's fever prescription. The same thing happened on Tuesday and Wednesday, though a few of his university friends did drop by at night. From the upstairs window, I saw him standing on the dark verandah, conspiring seriously, glancing at the closed door behind him.

Later, when I asked him what they wanted, he said, 'Nothing important. Just talking.'

'Are you guys planning something?' He and his friends sometimes went to, or even organised, random events like flea markets or art exhibitions – out of sheer boredom, I thought.

Sreenath threw his hands up and said, 'What's with you people? I told you it's nothing.'

'Did you guys kill someone?'

He slammed the door of his room. On it was a golden sticker of Lord Shiva and Ganesha saying 'Om'. I'd stuck it there a long time ago to annoy Sreenath. He'd changed the 'Om' to 'Ok' and let it stay.

On Thursday night, I ran into Salil as I was coming back from the paper. Salil was four or five years older than me and also lived with his parents in Blue Hills. He had a reputation for being rowdy – probably fuelled by the fact that he was always going somewhere even though he didn't have a job. Otherwise he seemed like a perfectly nice guy. This time, too, he was on his bike, an orange Duke covered in sponsorship decals. He pulled up next to me at the entrance of Blue Hills, and cut the engine with a show of reverence.

'How's your brother doing?'

My brother wasn't friends with Salil, so I was surprised that he knew to ask. I was even more surprised by his grim expression. Did he think Sreenath had malaria or dengue?

'It's nothing major,' I said.

Salil frowned and nodded like I'd said something wise. 'That's the spirit.'

I blinked. 'What is?'

'Your parents are okay with him, though?'

'*Okay* with him? How do you mean?'

He stared at me.

'It's all good, then,' Salil said. 'Great. That's good.'

Still thinking of malaria, I said, 'He barely even had a fever to begin with.'

'Right. Good. Anyway.' Salil started his bike and said he had to hurry.

It was almost eleven.

When I got back to the house, Amma was the only one awake. I quickly ate dinner, helped her close the kitchen, and went to bed, feeling odd.

3

It was on Friday evening that things started to unravel. I came home early after watching a play for the paper. While I still had the review to submit, I didn't want to jump in right away. The theatre had had a full house despite the play being billed as experimental. The tenacity of the crowd had lightened me up and made me feel as though the city was secretly full of sophisticated people, all with rich inner lives. When it started raining, I sat by the window in the living room, sipping tea and scribbling in a notepad. I heard Sreenath's footsteps above me.

It had been half an hour since Amma left for the Blue Hills society meeting. She always took great care to dress well before she went to one of these. If any of us were around, she'd ask a hundred questions to which she already knew the answers. Should she take an umbrella? Would she need her purse? Did her hair perhaps look *too* black?

She treated these meetings like they were job interviews.

Appa came home at six thirty, just as I finally started typing out the review. He was early as well. After asking me where Amma was and what I was doing, he went upstairs to take a bath and, a few minutes later, called me to the bathroom.

Appa had a frozen shoulder from all the lifting he still insisted on doing at the warehouse. His baths had become two-man operations. Midway, he'd summon Sreenath or me – mostly, me – and make us wipe down his back while he sat on a wooden stool, wearing a towel. Sometimes he'd listen to the radio on his phone.

The cramped bathroom was full of steam. A yellow light bulb floated above it. I grabbed a sponge and focused on the suds circling the drain. No luck with the radio.

'Is it okay for Sreenath to miss an entire week at the firm?' Appa asked.

'I don't know. He must have talked to them.'

'He told me they said it was okay. But I wouldn't like it if one of my employees took off for an entire week. Who's going to do all his work?'

'They must have people, Appa.'

'Then what's the point of having him there at all?'

Conversations with Appa usually exacerbated all my parental worries. No disrespect, but I didn't like the idea that all they thought about were these domestic things. Seeing if I could provoke the inner life I mentioned earlier, I tried to make them watch interesting films on TV, at least once in a while. I even tried to take Amma to a play once, a Malayalam production of Chekhov's *Uncle Vanya*. She couldn't have cared less. It wasn't that I considered myself a great intellectual; I just wanted what was best for them, and even though this may sound silly, I didn't want to feel like they'd been left entirely unprepared for life's big questions.

As Appa talked about Sreenath and then his own day, getting more and more agitated, I tried to maintain my earlier equilibrium. A while later I heard the front door open and Amma come in. It was seven when I went downstairs.

Usually when Amma returned from these meetings, she'd talk at the rate of ten to twelve words a second – what was new, what people had said. That evening I found her in the kitchen staring at the numbers on the microwave.

'Amma, good meeting?'

She said yes without turning around.

I left it at that, went to the living room, and sat down at the dining table to work again. Maybe somebody had said something rude to her, I thought. Maybe she had a headache.

Amma came in five minutes later and walked slowly to the window. In succession, she closed the curtains completely, opened them wide, and then, seemingly after some calculation, adjusted them so they were exactly as they had been before. She hovered over to where I was sitting.

I'm not sure how to describe this correctly, but all her features were slightly displaced. Her eyes had bored in deeper. Her mouth was slack. Her forehead looked bigger. There was no colour on her face. I had the sensation of being in the room with a stranger, so much so that I remembered those ghost stories where people saw pale images of their loved ones without realising they'd died a few minutes earlier.

'Did Sreenath say anything to you?' she asked.

'About what?'

'Don't lie. Did he?'

'I don't know what you're talking about, how can I lie?'

'Is he here?' Amma turned around to look at the stairs.

'Will you tell me what's wrong first?'

She turned back to me with a baffled expression and said, 'Poornima told me the strangest thing just now. You know what she's like. She *has* to dig up something or the other. Remember when Sreenath passed one of his papers and she said she was going to recommend chartered accountancy to all her nephews? Like it was so easy?'

Poornima aunty lived on the other side of Blue Hills. Our neighbours weren't fundamentally evil or anything. It was a small community, is all.

'I don't understand,' I said. 'What exactly did she say?'

Amma squinted and rubbed the tip of her nose like someone had swapped it out without her knowing.

'I'm sure it's nothing. It's just what she's like. But what she said was that there's a bad video of him online.'

'Of Sreenath?'

Amma nodded. 'With some girl, apparently. They all know about it, it seems. Very strange.'

'Online where?'

Then just like that, she stopped looking puzzled and started crying. It happened so fast, I wondered if I'd missed a second. I had seen Amma cry many times before, but this was different. It looked like her whole face was sliding downwards and turning into goo.

I made her sit down at the table and poured her a glass of water. Amma tried to talk but gasped instead. Finally, in answer to my question of 'where', she said, 'It's on one of those websites.' Saying this seemed to have cost her a lot of energy. She leaned forward on the table, hands on her head.

I tried to calm her down by pretending to scold her in my rational voice. I often used this voice with her. Our home, like many homes in the city I'm sure, had a proclivity for soap-opera moments. You couldn't get by without a rational voice.

'Have you seen this video yourself?'

I said 'video' in a mocking way, as though the very existence of moving pictures was a ludicrous concept.

Amma nodded no.

'Then it could easily be a misunderstanding.'

'It's not.'

'Of course it could be a misunderstanding. We'll speak to Sreenath. He'll clear this whole thing up. Simple.'

I was kneeling on the floor now, talking to her like she was a child, as pieces from the past few days clicked together in my head. Then I was thinking about what Appa would say. Next thing, he was standing in the living room.

Appa was wearing only a lungi. A white towel was draped across his shoulders. Understandably, he looked alarmed. He'd already been complaining of a bad day. One of his oldest employees had threatened to quit, and his sister had called to reignite a property dispute. In the bathroom earlier, Appa had vigorously scratched his whole upper-body like ants were crawling all over him. 'For a single morsel of peace, should I have to go to the Himalayas and meditate for a hundred years?'

Seeing him now, Amma started crying twice as hard.

Appa turned to me like I was responsible. 'What is all this?'

13

I told him I didn't know, which was the best I could do right then. With all the crying, even I was starting to panic. Amma's situation was worse. The more she cried, the more Appa shouted questions; the more he shouted, the more she cried.

After two minutes of this, Amma began telling him what she had told me. I decided to check on Sreenath – he still hadn't made a sound – and went upstairs and knocked on his door.

'Sree, just come out here for a second and clear this up.'

No response.

'Sree, Amma is saying there's some sort of video online. Do you know anything about this?'

No response again.

Now I grew worried that he might have done something to himself. I knocked harder.

'Hello hello. Sree. Are. You. There.'

Eight or nine knocks in, he said, 'Stop doing that. I'll come down in a bit.'

His voice sounded light and distant.

'Do you know anything about a video?'

'I told you,' he said, like he was speaking through his teeth now. 'Just give me a few minutes.'

By then Appa was already stomping up the stairs. He pushed me aside and pressed himself against Sreenath's door. Whatever Amma had told him, she must have done so in more detail than when she had told me.

'Do you know what they are talking about?' he asked. 'Is it true?'

When Sreenath didn't respond, Appa looked confused at first and then angry. He started banging on the door, calling his name again and again. In his half-naked state, Appa was like a frog, croaking. 'Sreenath' lost all meaning and, as he kept repeating it, went from being a name to being a disturbing noise.

I thought for sure Appa was going to have a heart attack. Appa's heart attack was like that Californian earthquake, the Big One. It was always on its way. He threatened us with it every time we did something that annoyed him.

'Appa, calm down,' I said. He ignored me. I took a few steps forward, but he held up a hand to warn me off.

I can't remember how long Appa stood there or how many times he called Sree's name but I'm inclined to say forty or fifty, even though that sounds like a lot.

When Appa finally stopped, it was because he needed the extra energy to start kicking the door.

'Open this right now,' he said.

This change, even if it was an escalation, actually made me feel better. At least it proved Appa's head was still functioning.

Behind me, Amma was standing on the stairs, taking shallow breaths. I made her cross over to the landing, afraid she'd faint and fall down. That too and the evening would have been complete.

Meanwhile, Appa had started kicking the door even harder. Not even Amma, who usually ruled over the household decibel output, was brave enough to stop him.

'I want to see this video,' he was saying. 'I want to see the video now.'

'Appa, please,' I said. 'He'll come out. He told me he'll come out in a minute.'

'Send me the video right now or I'm breaking this and coming in.'

'Sree,' I shouted. 'Tell him you'll come out.'

When the next kick landed, the bottom part of the door made a loud crack.

Appa adjusted his lungi and wiped his mouth.

Maybe Sreenath wanted to get all this over with in one go.

From the other side of the door, he said, 'I have sent it to you. It's on WhatsApp.'

I noticed that he sounded calm now. Calmness was good, but in general, incongruity was not.

Appa waited for a second to see if Sreenath would say anything else, then went down followed by Amma. I put my ear against the door and remained still. The bed creaked. I recognised the flexing of Sree's chair and the sound of him typing on his laptop. Downstairs, everything had become quiet. They must have been watching the video.

When I finally went to the living room, Appa and Amma were both sitting on the sofa. Amma was stroking Appa's arm.

While Appa did have a temper, I couldn't recall an outburst as worrying as the one that had just happened. Of course, they weren't the type to be quietly angry or even passively aggressive. Shouting wasn't uncommon, and when that didn't work, flying cups, saucers and plates were all part of the vocabulary. I don't want to give the impression that we were crass. It's just that no one had time to be subtle.

Appa's phone was on the teapoy. I unlocked it and stared at the paused video. The fact that he didn't even have a password made me sad. With Appa, what you saw was what you got.

Unsure how all this was going to turn out, or maybe just wanting to make myself useful, I went to the kitchen and hid the sharp objects I could find. Since I had the phone with me, I played a portion of the video, not really looking at it. With such a shocking prelude, the content shouldn't have surprised me, but it still did a bit.

I forwarded the video link to my phone, went to the bottom of the stairs and sat down. The house was silent. Not to be too poetic, but I could still hear, floating around me, all the things that had been shouted so far.

When half an hour passed and no one had moved, I texted some excuse to my editor at the paper, went back upstairs and knocked on Sreenath's door.

'Sree, it's only me,' I said. 'Open the door, da.'

The door opened. The room was small enough that he could do the latch with his toes while sitting at his desk. Sreenath had his laptop in front of him and was typing on his phone with double thumbs. The air was hot and smelled like wet coins. It was dark. Only his table lamp was on.

'Why didn't you tell me?' I asked.

'Then what?'

'I don't know. What are we supposed to do now?'

He shrugged and kept texting.

'What the fuck,' I said. 'You didn't have to see them. I did. They look like they are dying.'

16

'I need to be alone right now,' he said.

'And do what?'

He got up and opened the door. I refused to move. He put a hand on my collar and tried to throw me out. I pushed him back against the wall. He managed to wriggle free and tripped me with his foot.

'All right, fine,' I said.

I stepped outside. The door closed once again. I went to my room and sat on the bed.

4

I had only seen Anita, Sreenath's girlfriend, twice. Both times it was when he made me take Appa's scooter and drop him off at the bus stand where they were meeting. They had gone to the same university and studied commerce in the same batch. Sreenath had started dating her at the beginning of his second year, though he didn't say anything to me till they'd been together for over six months.

The first time I saw her, Anita was leaning against a signpost and digging in her backpack. She was wearing a white T-shirt and blue jeans. Her glasses had rectangular plastic frames, and her hair was pulled back into a ponytail.

I'd just finished school then. And the few girls I knew were the ones I added on Facebook. These were random students from around the city. I did chat with some of them but only on the level of pleasantries and schoolwork.

'Will you please stop staring like a fish,' Sreenath said. He walked towards Anita.

Together they crossed the road but timed it badly. A packed bus had to slam its brakes and honk at them. They froze for a second, right in the middle; and then, once on the other side, slinked into an old coffee house looking very red.

The next time I saw Anita was several months later on a rainy evening. The bus stand was crowded. She was all the way at the back wearing a translucent raincoat, earphones in, and lightly tapping her wet Converse to music.

While I didn't meet her on either occasion, I did get an *idea* of her over time. Anita enjoyed reading. Through Sreenath, she borrowed books from me like *Less Than Zero* and *Cloud Atlas* and *The Name of the Rose*.

Sreenath and I both liked to read, though I think I was more consistent. It's hard to be sure because Sree's books always stayed in his room along with the rare magazines he somehow found: *The Illustrated Weekly* from back when Khushwant Singh used to edit it, *Himal Southasian*, *Life*, *Mad*, *Atlantic Monthly*.

My personal book collection wasn't huge by any means. Unless it was required by syllabus, Appa had always made us use the public library. Any books that I did own, I'd scored second-hand. This went on until I joined university for my communications BA and the course became much too vague for anyone to track.

When Anita wanted books from me, I was happy to be included. I think Sreenath too was secretly proud to say we had them at home, even if they weren't all very niche.

The other book she'd borrowed was Daphne du Maurier's *Rebecca*. That came back with wrinkled edges and an apology note addressed to me. Written in careless loops, it said: *I'm really sorry – I spilled a glass of water on it while reading. I couldn't get the same edition on Amazon, but I'll replace it as soon as they have it in stock. Thank you so much.*

'She dropped it in the bathroom.' Sreenath had already told me this, missing the note. I told him she didn't have to buy me a new copy. The book was old anyway and I'd read it before. Even so, a new one arrived a few weeks later. This time the note said: *Okay so I did drop it in the bathroom, but Mr Muscle and I do germ-genocide on a regular basis and it was only on the floor and not any place too unsanitary. Also, your brother tells me you're a toilet-reader too.*

In reply I told Sree to text her and say: *Thank you very much for the book, Anita. You really didn't have to. Yours truly,* Fellow Toilet

Reader. Sreenath groaned at my sign-off for about two minutes before finally pressing Send.

Another thing I knew about Anita was that she hated being home. I heard Sree mention it over the phone one day, in the context of a labour strike that kept getting prolonged.

There were no buses. All the shops were shuttered. Our universities had given us a break. The two of us were sitting in the living room, watching the news. A mob was burning an effigy.

Once Sreenath hung up, I tried to act cool: turned a page of a newspaper, checked the time, scratched my nose. I asked, 'Why does she hate being home?'

'Who *likes* being home?'

'Why doesn't *she* like being home?'

'This and that.'

'Like what? Schizo family?'

Sreenath yawned and said, 'When you use mental health lingo the way you do, you end up creating more stigma around it. You should know that by now.'

'I have plenty of schizo friends,' I said. 'My wife is a schizo.'

Sree ignored this and went to the kitchen. I figured he wasn't going to say anything more, so I let it be.

While Sreenath was doing his CA, I was told Anita was taking her Master's either in sociology, psychology or philosophy – he kept changing the details just for the sake of it. Occasionally, I overheard other facts. Like, way back in school, she used to quiz at the state level. She had a crush on the actor Fahadh Faasil. She posted cartoons and illustrations online and got a lot of likes. She co-edited a university magazine that was considered prestigious in certain circles.

One night, Sreenath told me: 'Anita used to believe aliens were going to take her away. When she was a kid.'

We were standing on the verandah during a power cut, staring at the sky and discussing conspiracy theories. On clear nights, the stars settled right down. Once again he quickly changed the subject. His dreamy tone made me wonder if they were in the middle of a fight. Usually during our power cuts, Sreenath just scrolled his phone.

Around that time, I developed the habit of scribbling *Anita believes in aliens* or even *Annie believes in aliens* in the margins of my notebooks. That was my brain's screen saver. I wrote it whenever I was bored. *Annie believes in aliens.* To me that phrase was mysterious and attractive. A girl looking up at the sky, hoping for salvation. I would have liked to know more, but he didn't mention the aliens again.

In fact, aside from some other basic biographical facts, and whatever I got from Anita's Instagram page, this was all I knew about her.

I didn't think Sree's reticence meant she was unimportant to him, though. Only that he was protective of her. Sreenath could go on about the big picture – politics, music, the Adoor Gopalakrishnan retrospective he'd caught at IFFK. But he always kept quiet about the things he really considered precious. I thought they were in love.

One thing I learned about Sreenath after he got together with Anita was that he could be romantic. I was surprised by this – I couldn't imagine anyone in our family being romantic. I also felt somewhat proud of him precisely because it was like he'd defeated some genetic destiny. Sree had all these mementoes: ticket stubs, food bills, foam coffee cups, a strapless watch dial, a scrunchie. He kept them in his desk drawer.

One Saturday morning when guests were due, Appa became possessed by a cleaning fit. It started in the living room but soon he was going into cupboards and coming out from under the beds. In Sreenath's room, Appa threw away the mementoes, thinking they were junk. When Sreenath returned from university, he was livid.

'Why did you have to clean in here?' he shouted. 'I told you not to do it!'

'Your room is what, an embassy?' Appa said. 'It's part of the house, isn't it?'

Thankfully, the coffee cups, the watch dial and the scrunchie were still in the waste bin. It was too late to salvage the rest. Sreenath took what he could back to his room and put them exactly where they had been before.

'Yes, take more garbage,' Appa said. 'Fill your whole room with it.'

Amma brought up the scrunchie later, trying to gather intelligence by asking Sreenath, jokingly, if he planned to grow his hair. He acted like he hadn't heard her.

Later, when I was asked, I said, 'Do you think he tells me?'

That made her smile.

When the video happened – its discovery, that is – Sree and Anita must have been together for about four years. At first, I'd assumed it would be something they recorded themselves, which then got leaked. The actual thing showed them outside, in a frame of grass and thick trees. It was twelve minutes long and seemed to have been filmed from behind some bushes, into which the camera retreated once or twice. For the most part, they are sitting on the ground next to each other, their backpacks on either side, their backs against a tall rock. Anita is wearing a WWF T-shirt and tracksuit bottoms. Sree is in their university's blue-white uniform. While they weren't having sex, what they were doing was sex-adjacent, essentially third base. Towards the middle, Sreenath exposes himself for nearly a minute.

Sitting on my bed that evening, I spent a long time staring vacantly at banner ads for extra performance and penis enlargements. I stared at them so long, they must have thought, Wow, this guy is actually considering it.

The site itself wasn't one of the famous ones but the video had close to 100,000 views. There was a date in the description that said it had been uploaded a year ago. Using trigonometry on Sreenath's cropped hair, his Puma sneakers and his uniform, I could tell it had been filmed even before that, when he was around twenty and in his final year. I couldn't identify the location in the video right then, but later I learned that it was a moppy hilltop not too far from their university. Desolate, though not desolate enough, clearly.

Hometown romance sometimes led you to strange places. A

classmate of mine, a seminary-aspirant named George, used to joke that it was only a law of physics: any vacuum that offered privacy was filled sooner or later by a couple. There were spots on the beach, for instance, where late in the afternoon you might see umbrellas facing the horizon, inside each one, a couple. Granted, most of them were probably only kissing or holding hands, nothing more.

I closed the page and put my phone away. On the whole I felt irritated with everyone: Sreenath, Anita, my parents. I also had questions. Had Sreenath known about the video for a year and just kept quiet about it? Who filmed it? Had people from his university come across it recently? Two of his juniors lived in Blue Hills. One of them was Mrudula aunty's daughter. Mrudula aunty was close friends with Poornima aunty.

I imagine that when she told Amma about the video, she must have said something about it being her duty. She really must have felt that way too.

Amma herself had used that line before, when she'd found a society resident's daughter buying rum with her friend at BEVCO. This girl used to look depressed as it was, the way she walked around Blue Hills. I got annoyed at Amma for telling on her.

'She's just nineteen,' Amma had said, defensive. 'It's not a good habit. It's drinking now. What's next?'

What *was* next? Drugs? Partying? Sex? Eyes Wide Shut? I don't mean to sound like I'm making fun of Amma; that's just the way things were.

'Maybe you should have just talked to the girl instead of going straight to her mother,' I said. My mother talking to her would have been disastrous, actually. The girl probably would have said something smart and made her cry till it was 2040.

'I explained to her mother that, look, it happens sometimes,' Amma said. 'Some teenagers go through this at one time or another. All you have to do is keep an eye on her. That's all.'

Sreenath, who had been reading the paper, sighed, got up and left the room. He must have been thinking about glass houses. Sreenath was an occasional drinker himself, and when he got

23

the chance to drink properly, he would get so plastered, his eyes would roll away from each other. Even I drank every now and then, if the circumstances were favourable and the company was good. Afterwards, I would swallow equal parts mouthwash and spray deodorant on myself like I was in an Axe commercial.

5

Sex was one thing; a sex scandal was another thing altogether. That Friday, the house was full of volatile stillness. Appa and Amma stayed in the living room for a long time doing nothing. The porch lights remained off till Amma decided this would make us stand out too much. The rain had passed. Some of our neighbours were walking outside.

Meanwhile, I paced inside, dividing my time between the landing in front of Sreenath's door and the living room. I was afraid to say anything and, except for a few mumbled words, my parents were mainly stunned too.

At nine, Amma moved to the kitchen. From the living room, where I'd sat down next to Appa, I could hear her rummaging through the drawers. I was deciding whether or not to return her knives – and one particularly lethal peeler – when Sreenath came down.

He hesitated at the bottom of the stairs. For a second I thought he might say something. Instead he went to the kitchen. I heard cupboards being opened and closed.

Appa had seen Sreenath as well. Now the noise of the cupboards seemed to be getting on his nerves. Partly because it was Sreenath who was doing it and partly because, by doing it, he was aggravating one of Appa's bigger peeves. Appa was always accusing us of slamming doors too hard or crashing callously on to the sofa. He felt this showed a lack of respect for comforts that were hard-won.

I got up and went to the kitchen door. Sree didn't acknowledge me. More cupboards were plucked open and shut, though I doubt he was being provocative or even especially loud.

Amma was standing by the gas stove. I don't know what kind of far-fetched scenario was going through her mind, but she asked, 'Was there somebody making you do this?'

'I'm sorry, okay?' Sree said. He turned around and looked in Amma's direction. 'Just give me some time please.' He opened and closed a few more cupboards.

While this might make it seem like we have ten thousand cupboards at home, Sree was just going through the ones he'd already searched. I don't think he was paying any attention.

After still more searching, during which Amma only stared at him, he settled on a blue tin of chocolate biscuits.

'Were you forced into it?' Amma asked.

Sreenath scratched his jaw and looked at the ceiling like he was annoyed.

'Please, Amma. Do we have to do this now?'

Amma's eyes began welling up.

'Do you really have to cry so much,' Sreenath said. 'Has somebody died?'

This was just the sort of thing Appa was waiting to hear. He launched himself from the living-room sofa and shot through the kitchen door.

'Oh here he is, the great film star himself.'

'I can't do this,' Sree said.

'Why not? This is great. I expect we'll all be very rich soon. How much are they paying you for your role? One crore? Two? You know what time I came home from work yesterday? Four in the morning. Do you know what four in the morning looks like?'

'I'm tired,' Sree said, his voice drawn with a ruler. 'You are being ridiculous and unreasonable, Appa. I'm not in the space for this right now.'

This was a tactic that Sreenath sometimes used: he'd act indifferent and dismissive until Appa or Amma calmed down. That night I thought it was flawed in its application. I wasn't even sure if it *was* a tactic.

'You're not in the space for it?' Appa said. 'What space do you need? Do you want me to build you a shopping mall?'

Appa noticed the tin Sreenath was holding. 'Oh good. You found refreshments. Good good. Do you need anything else? Some chips? A drink, maybe?'

Sreenath flushed and put the biscuits down.

'Out there in the open,' Appa said. 'Behaving like some worthless animal. Aren't you ashamed?'

Now Sree started shouting. 'Why should I be ashamed? I'm not ashamed. I didn't rape anyone or steal anything. You can all go to hell.' In English, he added: 'Fucking piece of shit. Fuck you. Fuck this.' He enunciated these last two words with such force, it was like he'd climbed a mountain and planted a flag.

Appa clearly wasn't expecting such a reaction. In its place, he might have expected some grovelling even. It was true that, of the two of us, Sreenath was the one who talked back to Appa the most, but this was on a different level. I wanted to drag Sree up to his room. Of course what he said was *fundamentally* right – it wasn't like he'd done anything heinous – but I still thought it was stupid of him not to see the situation from our parents' point of view. They were the type who had to change the channel if they saw people getting romantic while one of us was around – sometimes it didn't even have to be people; once it was Bugs Bunny and his rabbit girlfriend. A long hug could make them uncomfortable. While attending Sreenath's graduation, I'd watched Appa and Amma turn red seeing a girl sitting on a guy's leg, posing for a photo. And it wasn't just them; this was the case with most people in their circle, most people in the city even. They were in shock.

'Get out before I do something to you,' Appa said.

Sreenath grabbed the biscuits again and went up the stairs. I thought the least he could do was hurry along. Instead, he took his time and even checked his phone.

When his door closed, Appa walked to the hallway and sat down on the floor.

'Appa, he's just tense,' I said. 'He's going through a lot. It's not easy for him.'

'We just bought that car,' Appa said.

For the first time in my life, it looked like he would cry. I didn't know what to do. He still hadn't put on a shirt after his bath that evening. To me, he went from looking like a frog to looking like a caveman out in the cold: incapable of thought or language, only emotion and incomprehension.

'Appa, please,' I said, squatting down next to him. 'This is just part of life. Things like this happen sometimes. You just have to take them in your stride.'

Amma, who hadn't stopped crying herself, sat down in the other corner of the hallway, a few feet from Appa. I looked at her for help, but she wasn't even on the planet any more.

I think I must have rattled off fifty platitudes in under a minute – from 'This is when you should show real character' to 'Life's just a big joke, Appa. You can't take it too seriously.' I don't think Appa listened to a word I said. Two or three minutes later, he took a deep breath and walked away.

When I got up, my throat was aching. I went to Sreenath's room and knocked on his door.

'That was bullshit, you know,' I said. 'What's wrong with you? Don't you have any empathy?'

He didn't say anything.

'Sree, let me in. We'll just talk this through and figure it out.'

'Can you figure out how to fuck off?'

I banged on his door a couple more times. 'Fuck you,' I said. 'Fuck. Off.'

'Be alone in there. I don't care.'

I went downstairs, made Appa, Amma and myself some tea. I was the only one who drank it. Later I fell asleep in the living room with the lights on.

6

In the beginning of my first year at university, I was buoyed by Sreenath's success with Anita and asked a classmate if she wanted to get coffee. Her name was Fiona, and the reason I liked her, aside from the fact that she was cute, was that she seemed as nervous as I was walking around campus.

On our first outing, I narrated not only my entire life story but also the plot of two blockbuster Malayalam movies and a novel. Fiona went the other way. She must have said ten or eleven sentences in total, not counting her order to the waiter. Maybe she was bored, I don't know, or maybe I had failed to convey the fact that this was a date. The whole time we were together, I got the feeling that she was waiting for me to get to the point: offer her a job, push insurance, give her a medical diagnosis. We didn't go out again.

Fiona eventually became a pianist in the university band and even played as a forward, my same position, for the women's football team. Maybe I should have waited till second year to ask her out, the way Sreenath had done it. For the rest of university, we smiled at each other, but acted like that outing had never happened. Every time I saw her, I imagined us raising a pen of football players and felt a dull pain.

Anyway, this was more or less my official dating record, and though it looks comically vacant, as far as I know, I was the rule, not the exception.

My only other significant experience was something I was pretty proud of. It was also far more unusual in that it had happened with a guy, a school friend of mine and a fellow topper in history who sometimes sent me torrent links to movies and music. His university was in Delhi but he'd come home for a week because his grandfather had died running the 10k 'Get Moving' marathon. My friend and I were in an upstairs bedroom in his family's old house. His parents, also visiting, were asleep downstairs. We were done with a large bottle of vodka and two hours of a horrible jazz documentary when he started talking about massage parlours in Delhi that offered happy endings and how much happy endings cost, and would I like one for free?

If I've learned anything from Appa, it's to recognise a good deal.

The next day, I was euphoric. To be clear, I was then and still am on the straight end of the spectrum, so the euphoria wasn't about some sudden sexual awakening.

One reason I was so happy was that my friend and I were completely normal with each other. What he said about the night before was: 'I hope that wasn't weird for you.'

And what I said was: 'Nah.'

'Cool,' he said. 'I'm bi. By the way.'

'Cool,' I said. There was none of that 'Please keep this to yourself' or 'It was a mistake' or 'Man, I was so drunk, I can't remember anything ha ha' business.

Another reason I was happy was that I myself felt no guilt or worry or confusion whatsoever. I'd gone with the flow. To me, this was evidence that I wasn't some small-town rube.

Back home, lying in bed for a mid-morning nap, I heard the washing machine downstairs, Appa and Amma sifting for some lost documents, Sreenath shouting, 'Did someone use my Mach3 to shave their armpits? The blade is –' I looked outside my window and saw the tops of coconut trees and felt I'd pulled a fast one on everybody. I also figured something like this counted twice as much as any experience Sreenath had ever had, since it was rarer and more sophisticated – though of course I didn't tell him.

On the whole, it was like I was about to enter a kind of elevated existence.

The morning after I first watched Sreenath's video was the opposite. It was a Saturday. Everything was wrong. I could see from where I was lying on the sofa that Amma was glaring at the dishes in the kitchen sink. I pretended to be asleep, then dropped off once again. If I'd hoped for improvement the next time I woke up, I was promptly disappointed. Amma was still in the kitchen, still glaring at the dishes. Usually, we'd have long finished tea by now, but nobody was around and I don't think Amma had even opened the door to get the milk. It must have been around eight.

I had work that morning, but the paper was relaxed about interns. The editors didn't even like us visiting the office because it was overstaffed. I got two or, at most, three assignments a week – and they weren't going to win anybody a Pulitzer. As much as I wanted to leave the house and imagine from afar that things were improving, I felt it was best if I stuck around and spoke to Sree first.

The night before, I'd googled ways to remove videos from the web. Going by what most forums and blog posts were saying, the situation seemed bleak, especially when it came to the smaller, shadier sites. On an instinct, I'd then googled the video's title and found copies in three more places. Two of them opened. One needed a VPN. These were just the copies under that particular title, who knew how many there were in total.

I thought all this was world-class research that would help me and Sreenath get talking once he was awake.

In the meanwhile, I got up and started my rounds in the kitchen.

'Where's Appa?'

'Sleeping,' Amma said. My arrival had prompted her to rinse a glass.

'Still?'

'Must be.'

I knew he and Amma had gone to bed early, but maybe they'd been up talking. I figured this was a good thing.

'Doesn't he have to go to the shop?'

'Don't know.'

'Where's Sreenath?'

'Don't know.'

'I think I'll take a shower.'

'Okay.'

'Amma, just say something.'

'What's there to say?'

'Have you spoken to anybody? Karthika aunty?'

Amma shook her head and sniffled.

'Are you okay?'

'Yes.'

Upstairs, Appa was still in bed, covered in a blanket from head to toe. Sreenath's door was shut. By the time I'd brushed and showered, Amma was in their bedroom too, looking out of the window.

I knocked on Sreenath's door as lightly as I could. He must have realised I wasn't going to stop so he opened. The way he did, it was like banging the door, but in reverse.

'I just wanted to see if everything was okay,' I told him.

Sree gave me an exaggerated shrug. His hair was bushed upwards, like he'd gone Super Saiyan. In his hand was an old newspaper, a prop likely.

I lowered my voice. 'What about Anita?'

'What about her?'

'Does her family know?'

'Nope.'

I figured even back then that Anita's family was going to be the next big problem.

'I'm skipping work today.'

'Okay.'

'Do you need help?'

'All good here.'

'I found more copies of the video.'

'Cool, thanks.'

For some reason, he saluted me, then closed the door.

'I'll be downstairs till you're awake,' I said.

That was that. The house was silent.

What happened next always seems slightly silly to me. Not *what* happened actually, but the *way* it happened.

After leaving Sreenath in his room, I waited downstairs for someone to make an appearance. Nobody so much as talked. Finally around nine, I stepped out to call my editor and walk a few laps. I must have been gone ten minutes tops. By the time I got back, there had been a shake-up.

Appa was sitting in the living room, staring at the paper. Amma was at the dining table with a glass of water.

'Everything okay?'

Nobody answered me. I asked again.

Appa cleared his throat and turned a page. 'Yes,' he said. 'Great.'

I went upstairs. Sreenath's door was open. Several of his clothes were missing. Also gone were his laptop and his course books.

I hurried back to the living room. 'Where's Sreenath?'

'I told him to get out,' Appa said.

'When? Get out and do what?'

'I told him to go live somewhere else.' Appa was still looking through the paper.

I turned to Amma.

'Did Sreenath do something?'

'He's done enough,' Appa said. 'I'm not wasting my life on him.'

'This isn't the time to be angry, Appa. This is not sensible. Where's he even going to go?'

'Not my concern. He can camp outdoors for all I care. He seems comfortable there anyway.'

I nearly punched a wall before going upstairs and dialling Sree's phone. There was no answer. I kept trying all morning.

Later that day, I found out more about Sree's flash eviction from Amma. When I'd stepped out, both Appa and Sree heard the door and opened their doors to see if it were the other leaving. Appa began to taunt Sreenath. Annoyed, Sreenath said he was going for a walk. Appa said, 'You have shamed us enough. Now you want to parade yourself to the entire colony?' Sreenath replied, 'I'm going outside to find more women and make more videos.' Appa slapped him and issued an ultimatum saying he couldn't come back in if he took one step outside. Five minutes later, Sree took several, leaving the house with an old duffel bag.

Amma told me all this like she had only stood around watching, but I'm sure she must have said this or that. Her involvement in arguments between Sree and Appa usually made things worse. Usually, Appa and Amma would take off on their own tangent. Somewhere along the way, I would get involved. Weeks would go by. Finally Appa would give in and try to make amends. Amma would hold out. Appa would call her a feminist. Amma would get offended. 'Would a feminist make you three meals a day and snacks?' Another fight would begin.

That afternoon, I tried explaining Sreenath's frame of mind to my parents through two separate doors that were locked – Appa was in their bedroom by then; Amma was in Sree's room, raiding his cupboards. What I believed was that Sree wasn't being stubborn or rude or unapologetic: he was just flustered.

Nothing doing.

I even tried making vague philosophical points. Didn't Appa's niece call just last month to share the news about her having a baby? Wasn't she practically telling the whole world that her husband, the respected banker, had done a variation of what Sreenath had done, and done it so well that he had created new life? We didn't shame them, did we? We went over with sweets. What about that?

I didn't say it so crudely, but either way, nobody was interested. This was real life.

Towards the evening, Appa and Amma started arguing. Amma's reaction to Sreenath getting kicked out was squashed by Appa's anger and accusations that she was the one who always pampered Sree, she was the one who gave him all that extra pocket money, she was the one who supported his decision not to retake the engineering entrances, and she was the one who let him be a lout in the name of studying chartered accountancy.

This fight about education was an old one, probably common across the country. I wasn't lying earlier when I said Sreenath was smart – he really is – but things took a turn after his tenth grade. Sree had wanted to study humanities before university, but Appa and Amma had pushed him towards engineering and straight into a slump that lasted all through his eleventh and twelfth. This was made worse by Appa and Amma's suspicion that Sree was self-sabotaging, as opposed to what he insisted was the real problem: 'I just can't cope with the load.' It really was heavy. Five a.m. tuitions every day, schoolwork, homework, entrance coaching on weekends.

One morning, Sree and I had woken up to find that the cable and the internet had been disconnected to 'encourage concentration'. In the living room, Sree made a speech about why he needed the internet to study, called the house a concentration camp, and left for his friend Roshan's place where they enjoyed abundant quantities of BSNL broadband and everyone was happy in the twenty-first century.

And that's where he stayed, through two balmy nights and Roshan's mother's many polite questions, until Appa and Amma finally agreed to restore the internet but not the TV.

This was by no means a one-off. In fact, something or the other used to happen every week. It didn't help that our cousins, all of whom had also taken science like Sreenath, were doing so well it felt like they were succeeding just to spite us.

When two years passed and Sree's board results came, his scores were in the low sixties. Appa became obsessed with the idea of buying an aquarium and raising zebrafish. Amma told everyone that we were applying for a re-evaluation. Sree ended up studying commerce at a local university and, after that, chartered accountancy, which stranded him even further in Trivandrum.

Sreenath's academic tumble was something Appa and Amma often passed between themselves like a thorny ball. The other things Appa accused Amma of now – the pampering, pocket money – were blatantly false.

When fed up, Amma can deliver a frightening performance. As soon as Appa wound down, she said, 'Shall I go into the kitchen, turn the gas on and burn myself? Will that satisfy you? If I have been such a bad mother, is that enough atonement?' She was holding a matchbox. After that, Amma disconnected herself from the day's proceedings and started doing all the chores in the known universe, going so far as to dust the ceiling fans.

Around late evening, I took the scooter and went to the Goethe-Zentrum in Palayam. There were maybe twenty others in there watching a film. I found a seat at the back and sat down with my feet under me. The film was about a man who turns himself into a golden retriever after his wife dies. It was supposed to be a kind of meditation on grief. I sometimes wished my parents would express themselves in ways like that. Turn themselves into plants or animals, or maybe even do a modern dance.

Before long, I fell asleep, dreaming of strange shapeless things, and woke up only when Joy, the deputy director of the centre, was standing in front of me.

'Sir, the screaming is over,' she said.

I looked at her.

'The screening is over, sir.'

Sure enough, the audience had emptied out and the lights had been switched on.

'Sorry,' I said, blinking.

'Thank you for coming.'

I must have been there a zillion times but still there was no warmth from Joy.

Stepping outside, I plugged my earphones in and tried to reach Sreenath again.

On call number fifty-five or so, he answered. It was another twenty-four hours, almost, before he finally caved and told me where he was staying.

7

The next day I visited Sree at his new place for the first time.

As I left home, both Appa and Amma acted indifferent, though I'm sure they must have been glad to know he was okay, never mind where.

Sree wasn't staying too far away: give or take twenty minutes in traffic.

It was early evening. The houses in the neighbourhood were mildewed and dull and pressed too close together. You could have jumped from one terrace to the next until you cleared the area.

Since Sree didn't answer his phone, and whoever had numbered the lanes apparently picked them out of a hat, I had to park my scooter and walk around for a long time trying to find the address. In the end, I spotted a familiar car, an ugly blue Santro, that belonged to Arjun, a friend of Sree's. It was parked by a one-panel gate in front of a single-storey set in a small, marshy compound. Next to the front door, there was a stained-glass window you couldn't really look through. The worn doormat said 'Welco'.

I didn't have proper plans other than reconnaissance, but I hoped Sree was in a suggestible state of mind.

When I rang the bell, another of his friends, a guy named Joel, opened the door.

I'd figured Joel would be there. I liked him. He used to come home when Appa wasn't around. 'Aunty, how are you,' he'd tell Amma, hulking through the door and smiling sheepishly. Joel was a hundred kilos with an equally heavy voice. He did Tamil folk theatre and used to work with Sree on various unreleased podcasts. Sree was supposed to be his manager or maybe producer, I'm not sure, but once upon a time he'd helped Joel hold a one-man show in Kochi.

Sree's interests lay in that direction, among things like management, entrepreneurship, advertising, production and publishing – though he wouldn't share any specifics with me. Biannually, Appa would try to wheedle Sree into telling him. Usually during festival season when the shop was doing great and Appa was in good spirits. It never ended well. Appa really tried, mind you. He listened, asked questions, nodded along. Thirty minutes would go by before he scratched his ears and began explaining money vis-à-vis trees.

Joel seemed unsure about me being there, but not for more than a second or two.

'Hey, da,' he said. And then, grinning: 'Sree, it's your brother. We have finally been caught.'

I disliked this introduction but didn't say anything. Joel stepped aside to let me in.

Despite the way it looked outside, the inside of the house was freshly painted. Everything was so white and bare, it felt like I'd died and gone to heaven. The air was laced with turpentine. It went straight to the top of my nose and gave me an instant headache.

Sree was in the living room. I hadn't expected to find him alone but nor had I expected a dense population and, among them, Anita. To me Anita's presence was the biggest surprise.

Aside from her, Joel and Sree, there were four others: two girls and two guys. The guys were Sree's university friends – Arjun, the owner of the blue Santro, and Thomas. I was always hearing about Arjun because he liked to be angry and Sree thought he was this smart underachiever. His long hair was tied into a bun and he seemed to have a permanent smirk. Because of the hair and the existence of two other Arjuns in their class, this Arjun was called Arjun Samurai.

Thomas was more his friend than Sree's, I think, and I didn't catch him much after this. I had zero idea who the girls were. Altogether, it was a lot to take in and the only thing Sree offered was a wave.

'Hey,' I said.

Sree was still in the shirt he'd worn when he left home. It had a flaking picture of Mount Everest.

'Are you okay?' I asked.

He gave me a thumbs-up and said, 'Yup.'

Everyone was sitting on the floor, spread across two straw mats separated by an open newspaper. Sreenath was on the large mat by the entrance of the room and Anita was on the opposite one, her back against the wall. She looked the same as she did in the video, perhaps a bit older. Same ponytail. Same plastic glasses, rectangle frames. Having seen Anita in a way I wasn't meant to, it seemed to me like I was inappropriately intruding even now, just by being around her.

Anita waved to me. With my hand extended, I rushed across the room. It felt a little like I was charging to lance her.

'How are you?' I said, with a sad face.

Anita shook my hand. 'I'm okay, mostly. Thanks. You?'

'Just figuring things out, you know.'

We nodded at each other and I backed away from her until I realised I was standing in the middle of the room, and retreated to the edge. I tried to cast Anita as the toilet-reader or the cartoon-ist or the magazine editor or Sreenath's girlfriend rather than as the girl from the video.

Thirty seconds later, the group had forgotten that I existed. When I told Sree I wanted to speak in private, he said he'd come in a bit. I tried making eye contact with Joel but he only smiled. How long was a bit?

For the next half hour or forty-five minutes, everyone exchanged theories about some heist that had happened nearby: a few guys had drilled into a bank but seemingly stolen nothing.

There was lots of banter, and the overall joviality wasn't what I thought I'd find. Especially after breathing the thin air at home. For this reason, it seemed manufactured. Except for fiddling with her phone, locking and unlocking it, Anita seemed composed too. Not chatty, but not falling apart either. The longest she talked was when she went on a rant about two of her classmates, a couple who exchanged Facebook passwords and messaged their mutual friends pretending to be each other. The topic was stolen privacy.

'They were telling me this story thinking I'd find it very cute,' Anita said. 'When I told them instead that it was a bit horrible, what they were doing to their friends, they started going on about how it helped them *understand* each other better. They even said something about understanding the other *gender* better.'

No one reacted with the degree of exasperation Anita seemed to want, but Sree added, 'They called it body swapping.'

I walked around the house. It didn't have much furniture: a wooden dining table, a cracked plastic chair, a folded mattress. Sree's bag was thrown into the empty bedroom, where it had marked a comet tail through the dusty floor.

The video was only mentioned twice.

Once was when I heard Arjun address Sree and Anita as porn king and queen. This was said casually and received casually, as part of the general conversational flow. They seemed to be encouraging that sort of thing.

Then a while later, I heard Sree say something about Anita's mother and how her surveillance and short-leash policy had sometimes made it impossible for them to get any privacy, let alone a room – though, he didn't quite stretch it to the other end and try to blame the video on her.

Sree had said this in response to Anita getting a phone call from home. She'd left to talk outside. I'd heard him from the kitchen where I was standing around tired of waiting, annoyed to see they'd stocked up supplies as though for a prolonged stay.

*

Reconnaissance-wise, I had more success after I volunteered for a cigarette run with one of the girls.

Her name was Dhruti. She was doing her MA with Anita and Meghna – the other girl there – but they'd been friends before too, having run into each other at an inter-university festival. Dhruti was light-skinned with loose wavy hair that swept the top of her shoulders. She seemed to have a lot of energy and so did her small messenger bag. The strap on it said, over and over again: *Baggu Baggu Baggu Baggu Baggu*. On our way to the store, it seemed like she was skipping – Dhruti took long strides on short legs.

'This must be so difficult for you,' she said. 'How you coping?'

'Yeah, it's all a bit messed up,' I said. I decided not to melt, though. 'I'm more worried about Sree. Anita too.'

It was after six now, but the ground hadn't cooled yet and the clouds were still orange. All around us were shards of bottles and dirty grass, fertilised by a nearby sewer which famously overflowed every monsoon. The road was empty except for the occasional bike taking a shortcut.

About Anita, Dhruti said: 'She slept for like three days straight when she found out about this. But yeah, she is a trooper. Both of them are. They are fine.'

'I can barely get Sree on the phone.'

'There's been a lot going on. There was the house stuff, running around, and then today we went to the police station? A friend of mine works there. He's trying to take the video down. We'll see.' She clapped her arms to her side and shrugged as if to say she couldn't take credit just yet.

At the roadside store, Dhruti bought cigarettes and mints. I'd started asking her about Anita's family. I already knew that her mother was an accountant and her father was some kind of an insurance person. Dhruti told me they all lived in a big house in Pettah, Anita's grandparents included.

'I mean, her folks seemed okay to *me*, personally,' Dhruti said. 'I had dinner with them once and they were, what, normal? But when it comes to things like this, it's hard to say.'

The shopkeeper told Dhruti, 'You really shouldn't smoke, sister.'

'Yes, thanks, uncle.'

She asked me if I wanted a cigarette, lit two and passed one. Pixels of red gloss stained the white Marlboro filter.

'Phew,' she said, exhaling and letting her shoulders fall. 'I've been craving that for hours.'

Another thing I learned on the walk was that the house Sree was staying in belonged to Meghna's uncle. He lived in Qatar. The previous tenants had left a few months earlier and now it was waiting to be occupied again. In the meantime, it had been overrun. Before I'd gone out, I'd seen Meghna tell everyone again and again that they shouldn't make too much noise. She was lanky and gave the impression of flapping about as she talked. 'Guys, please: inside voices.' Each time she said this, she'd apologise for being such a librarian. The fact that she had to apologise only seemed to annoy her more, though. Finally she'd sat down and sulked.

When I got back to the house, only Sree and Anita were in the same place as before. The others were surrounding a parcel of snacks at the dining table. Dhruti gave the cigarettes to Anita and joined them. Now that she was alone, Anita looked much smaller. More so after she gathered her knees and became a ball.

I sat next to Sreenath on the floor.

'When are you coming home?' I asked.

I wasn't sure how Appa would react if he did, but getting Sreenath to return would have been the first step anyway.

'I'm done with that place,' Sree said. 'You know what he did before I left?'

'Amma told me. He slapped you.'

'I should have left a long time ago.'

'Sree, they don't know any better, but you do. Just come back and we'll figure it out.'

He shook his head. 'There's nothing to figure out. They are the ones who lost their minds. Hardly the way to respond.'

I didn't stop to argue about the right way to respond.

'That's the way they are,' I said. 'You know them.'

I looked at Anita for some kind of a pacifying comment, but she was busy with her phone. When she saw me staring, she said, 'I have an assignment due tomorrow. And I just found out that there's an entire section I haven't covered.'

Sree asked, 'Do you have time to do it tonight?'

'I really doubt it. I think I'm going to have to fail this one.'

'Is it the twenty per cent assignment?'

'Yup. Preethi is already after my life for being late with all her work.'

'I think she loves doing you favours. You're basically her pet.'

They went on like this for three or four minutes. I thought both Sree and Anita looked really smug, acting as though this submissions thing was the biggest problem they were facing and everything else was old news that didn't bother them.

I asked Anita if she had to go to university the next day.

'We only have assignments and the dissertation now. No one really goes.'

'Are you staying here?' I knew there was no chance of that, but I was hoping she might advise Sree to go home as well.

Anita had lit a cigarette and was in the middle of a really long drag. Finally, when she'd just about sucked all the air out of the room, she coughed and said, 'Nope. Just visiting.'

'Everybody's going home,' I told Sree.

He shouted towards the dining table: 'Joel da, why in heaven's name did you let this guy in?'

'He was very strong, da,' Joel shouted back.

Sreenath turned to me. 'Look, I'm fine here. Just leave me alone.'

'I found more copies of the video,' I said.

'You told me. I know about it.'

I gestured in Anita's direction and lowered my voice. 'What happens now? What happens when her family finds out?'

Anita said, 'Everybody just needs to calm down first. It'll be fine.'

By then Dhruti had drifted towards us holding an egg puff. She said to Anita, 'Maybe you should just tell them and get it over with, you know?'

Anita said, 'Dhruti, your mater and pater are nice charming people. So please don't pretend to understand the struggles of us common folk.'

'Fine. I mean, my parents are better than they used to be, but it's not all roses. It's not like I don't know. I still feel you should just maybe tell them and take a stand. That's how you get them to come around.'

'This is your Marie Antoinette moment,' Anita said. 'Dhruti Antoinette.'

Dhruti sighed, patted Anita's shoulder and went back to the dining table.

I said, 'Sree, you should just come home for now. That's like you taking a stand.'

'Fuck off.'

'Appa and Amma mean well. They really do.'

'Yes, I can feel that on my face. My ears are still ringing.'

Sree then went on to list other instances where our parents had been horrible: including but not limited to the time Appa walked out of a family trip stranding us on a hill called Leopard's Nest, the time Amma threw our Onam lunches in the waste bin, the engineering fiasco obviously, and the time Appa stopped talking to Sreenath because he'd attended an LGBTQ rally.

'Why are you putting your head in other people's business?' Appa had asked him. 'If something happens during these so-called rallies, will they take care of you?'

Sree had ended up calling him a homophobe. Appa thought this was some kind of a musical instrument, though he took it as an insult just the same.

I stayed quiet for a few seconds; then, in a tone that I thought was less heavy, said, 'Every family has problems, Sree. Even Tolstoy said that.'

'Then Tolstoy can live with Appa and Amma.'

I looked at Anita again, but, again, no support.

As for Sreenath's litany of complaints, what could I possibly say? There was no denying that these things had happened. Of course, I didn't believe he actually hated Appa and Amma as much as he made himself think he did right then. This was the same person who, only two or three years ago, used to stay up brainstorming marketing strategies every time our business hit trouble.

Anita stubbed her cigarette and said, 'I should really get going.'

Sreenath told me, 'I think it's time you went home too.'

I didn't respond but fished for scooter keys in my backpack.

Before Anita left, she pressed Sree into a long hug. I think for a few seconds I fell in love with her – or, rather, the idea of being in love with someone like her. To me, the hug seemed like the reaffirmation of some pact they had between them or maybe a gesture of resilience.

Sreenath told her to call when she reached home. She smiled and said bye to the room.

When I stepped outside, the orange clouds had disappeared. It was dark. I drove the scooter around for a while and even did some stray shopping. By the time I pulled into Blue Hills, I was exhausted. It was almost eight. Of all the houses, ours looked the dimmest. Amma was sitting at the dining table with a physics textbook. Appa was in the living room, watching some old Disney movie that happened to be playing. He had a weakness for that sort of thing.

'I just saw Sreenath,' I said.

'Okay.'

'He's not doing good. You should talk to him.'

'There's nothing left to say.'

On TV, a prince was chasing a horse.

I tried to talk to Appa a few more times. Amma went to the bathroom when she thought she might be next. I threw my arms up and left it at that.

Later that night, I sent follow requests to Dhruti, Meghna and Arjun – Joel, I already followed. Anita too. Hers was a public account anyway, mostly full of R. K. Laxman-style illustrations about campus life and politics, or detailed reviews of various art supplies. The page had close to eight thousand followers.

I scrolled all the way down. A few pictures of herself. None of her house. Nothing that would give me any more clues about her family.

II

The Internet Is
Not a Fridge

8

Over the days that followed, there was an underwater atmosphere in the house: soft speech and sluggish movements, a lack of light.

Appa skipped work and barricaded himself in the bedroom with bricks of folders and files. It became Amma's turn to sit in front of the TV and not talk to anyone. Even though I stepped outside every now and then to cover events for the paper, it still felt like we were under siege.

The day after I visited Sreenath, there was a farewell party for Trisha, a university friend of mine. Trisha was leaving her current internship for a more exclusive one in Bombay. Her uncle had pulled strings. After that, she planned to apply for a visa and bolt to some university in England. It had all been arranged.

Lying in bed, I found it hard not to imagine her getting off a plane and into a black cab. Old buildings, clean pavements, fast trains, polite people. Right then, what I wanted most was to move to another country. In my head, the problems we were facing, such petty nothings and needless confusion, could only balloon in a place like this.

By the time of the actual party, I had thought so much about leaving that I'd imbued Trisha with special properties. It was late evening and she seemed to glow against the low light. The party was outdoors, at the house in Kowdiar where Trisha and her parents lived. Hers was the TV advertisement kind of family.

Trisha sometimes said things like 'My mother is my best friend', and I pictured the two of them combing their hair together. Her father wasn't far behind either – he probably combed his hair with them too.

I wanted to take Trisha aside and ask her out. I could then call and text her in England. Her boyfriend stared at me. He was a paranoid man. If you spoke as many as three words to Trisha, he would become your best friend for free. I left when he sidled up and started talking about how we all ought to catch a movie together. The city seemed even smaller on my way back.

The next couple of nights, I could barely sleep. In the mornings I'd wake up annoyed and angry, kicking the blanket to the floor.

When you're in a situation like that, I suppose it's only natural for the mind to play tricks on you. Outside the window, our neighbours appeared happier than usual. The weather was peach. Flowers bloomed everywhere and gardens filled to the brim.

The teenage girls from No. 17, the same pair who'd always seemed allergic to sunlight and exercise, began playing badminton outside their house. Every day for an entire week, all you could hear was the shuttlecock being tocked from one side to the other. They played so much, you'd have thought they were going national.

People started taking more walks than usual too, all of them dressed in giddy colours as though for a summer festival. I also noticed them staring at our house every time they passed. We lived down a cul-de-sac on the backside of Blue Hills. Now, even those who lived in the front section widened their orbit to include us. It seemed like we'd become an exhibit.

These weren't just my observations; in fact, more than me, it was Amma who parted the curtains and muttered under her breath whenever she heard footsteps or voices.

Amma wasn't keeping well. The day after Sreenath had left, she called Appa's mother and her parents to make sure they didn't know anything. Then she called around Blue Hills pretending to track a missing parcel. I heard her speaking in an upbeat tone. Before hanging up, she'd ask, 'And how is everything else? All good?'

Later in the week, Amma forwarded a video on the Blue Hills WhatsApp group. It showed an octopus shaking hands with a scuba diver. She sent the message at around four p.m., but it was well after ten by the time somebody replied with a thumbs-up. In between, she put her phone through every form of abuse possible, going so far as to hide it under a sofa cushion and sit on it. I don't think the delay meant people were ostracising her or anything like that. Nonetheless, she couldn't help but read into it.

Considering Amma had cancelled all her tuition classes and even told the maid to skip our house, I assumed she wouldn't go to the weekly society meeting. But come Friday, she dressed up the way she normally did, maybe with more fuss than was normal, and even broke out her hundred-point questionnaire.

I asked her if she was sure about going.

'They are having a fundraiser meeting,' Amma said, adjusting her hair in the hallway mirror. 'They'll be expecting me.'

Two years ago, Amma and some of the other residents had set up an annual kitty for an underprivileged school in Vattiyoorkavu. She considered the fundraiser to be one of the most important things she'd ever done.

When Amma returned two hours later, I asked her how it went.

'Good meeting,' she said. 'Good first meeting.'

It was a few minutes later that I learned she had pledged fifty thousand rupees – about ten times what we usually gave and much more than what we could spare.

'Is Appa okay with this?' I asked.

She brushed me off, saying, 'What's the use of money? What's the use of stockpiling it?'

If that's what we were doing, this was the first time I was hearing about it.

Karthika aunty visited our house that night. The living room was a mess. Populating it were teacups with coins of residue at the bottom, splayed bags of oily snacks, flyers that had fallen out of newspapers, and also a steam iron.

I stood on the stairs, having heard the doorbell, and watched Amma clean up as fast as she could. It was raining outside. When she opened the door, Karthika aunty ran in, planted her umbrella on the floor, and turned to the living room without really being invited.

For ten minutes or so, she led a quietly attentive Amma through the scenic route – discussing the weather, the power cuts, a cabinet reshuffle – before coming to the topic of the donation.

'We can't accept it,' she said. 'It's not right.'

There was a pause. 'What's not right?'

'With everything that's been going on –' Karthika aunty hesitated. 'It's too large.'

'Nothing is going on, Karthika,' Amma said. I could picture her putting on a puzzled smile.

'It feels like you're not in the right frame of mind. That's all.'

When Amma didn't respond, Karthika aunty said, 'You did your best. Sometimes these sorts of things happen.'

Maybe this was meant to sound consolatory, but it also seemed to imply failure on Amma's part. The silence trailing it was so thick the Israelis could have used it to stop missiles.

That wasn't enough for Karthika aunty. She kept going and asked, 'Did you not see any signs?'

'Signs?'

'Did he have trouble at home? Had he been staying away for longer? Often such things can be traced to the company they keep.'

Amma didn't reply. How were you supposed to reply to that anyway? How could there be signs for something like this? It's not like Sreenath had run away to join al-Qaeda, that you could have caught him signing up for flying lessons one day and googling tall buildings the next.

'Where's he now?' Karthika aunty asked.

'Living elsewhere. On his own.'

'You did the right thing, given the circumstances. Even with my daughter –'

Amma interrupted her before she could eulogise her daughter. 'Listen, I'm a bit busy now with some business matters. Can I come over later?' Karthika aunty's daughter was studying medicine at AIIMS. Her photo had been in the paper with other rank-holders as part of a coaching institute's advertisement. *Vibrant Academy congratulates its students, India's brightest stars!*

'And I don't think the donation is too large. I was the one who set up the fund. A one-time donation like this can have a much bigger impact than a drip of several small-scale donations. I think everyone should reconsider the amount they are giving. I just wanted to set the meter. But yes, thank you for your concern.'

Now the silence came from Karthika aunty's end. All said and done, she was one of Amma's closest allies. It worried me to hear Amma being rough.

'I understand,' Karthika aunty finally said. 'That makes sense, yes.'

I heard the two of them getting up. They appeared in the hallway.

'Anyway,' Karthika aunty said. She held Amma's hands for a few seconds, as though offering condolences, then nodded to me and left.

It was no secret that Karthika aunty had always disliked Sreenath. She must have thought he was rude – never going out of his way to say hi, hello, nothing. Sree had also made fun of her daughter for organising a Blue Hills Halloween party and attempting to get all of us to go house-to-house saying 'trick or treat'. She'd just returned from her first semester at AIIMS then, and even I could tell she only wanted to present her smug face at every possible door to soak up compliments. 'You don't even have to wear anything elaborate!' she'd said.

Karthika aunty's visit wasn't without damage. Amma stopped making pilgrimages to Sreenath's room and seemed to relax more about not having him home. Once or twice, she did ask me things like 'Is he eating? Does he have someone to get him food?'

I told her, no, he was likely starving or dying from dysentery.

'Maybe he'll end up in some ragpicker's ring,' I said. 'Maybe you'll run into him begging outside some temple.' It was a ridiculous thing to say. Sree wasn't a lost five-year-old.

Amma said, 'If that's what he wants, that's what he'll do. I can't help it, can I?'

It was easy to mistake Amma for someone who was soft all the time. When it came down to it, though, not even very deep down, she wasn't *that* different from Appa. Couples who stay together and all that. They put a lot of stock into this life they'd built even if I could never believe it. I always thought they were only a word or two away from getting divorced.

9

Those days reminded me a lot of how things were before we moved into Blue Hills, when we used to rent a place in a shabby part of the city. We all hated living there. The house was ancient, with a sloping roof that nested palm civets, and switchboards that leaked current. The floor was mosaic and almost everything else was made out of damp wood. Jurassic insects surrounded us. Grasshoppers. Moths. Beetles you couldn't just flick away – they were so large you'd be crushing their hopes and dreams.

Appa and even Amma seemed like they were ten times as busy. During the day, Amma would work from home, doing online transcriptions for an overseas company that wired us dirhams. At night, she'd sit on the bed and check the shop's books while waiting for Appa to come home. Then they'd scheme till two or three in the morning. Who to approach at what bank. How to get an extension on the lease. What mistakes to avoid in the coming future.

We must have lived in that house for almost nine years, starting when I was a kid. For a long time it felt like things were going wrong and that we were sliding unstoppably. Appa sent us to school with flyers advertising special discounts for parents. We never handed them out. Well, I didn't. Sree sometimes thought it made his backstory more deep. He'd go to the class teacher and say, 'Ma'am, could I please distribute these? It would really help my parents.' Teachers loved him.

I did try to help in other ways. During tense discussions, I would sit at the dining table and annoy Amma with my suggestions. I stayed awake when everyone else did. Sometimes I played the lottery after school. I also had a phase when I stole stationery from my classmates and hoarded it because it made me feel calm. We were never *that* broke, to be clear. The official line was, we were managing resources to climb as high as possible. So I didn't see my parents begging. We never discussed going to a different school – one without a football ground or a theatre club or *Compulsory English in the Hallways*. If we really had to buy something urgent, we thought about it thrice but, in the end, did. This went on for several years.

And then, slowly but noticeably, there was an actual uptick. The business started doing better and our income steadied. We began to eat out once or twice a month. More people started coming to our house and we started going to theirs. Sreenath stopped joking about running away.

It wasn't just a matter of money, though. It was also about losing a kind of aura, becoming more relaxed and less vigorous, less scrappy.

The day we moved into Blue Hills was one of the best ones ever. The sense of expansion was such that Appa lay on the cold marble floor, shouting at the ceiling and testing the echoes. The house wasn't that much bigger than our previous one, but we must have felt we were escaping old skin and becoming better people. The windows were tall, the kitchen was modern, the air went down easy.

Before the move, Amma had got her face done at a proper salon. She greeted our neighbours, beaming. She even bought sweets and took them around to every single person in the colony, including the gardener and the security guards.

Later that night, as all four of us sat in the living room after dinner, Appa said, 'Growing up, this is the sort of house I pictured myself living in.'

'Whose idea was it?' Amma asked, grinning. 'Who was the one who pushed for it?'

Just like the car many years later, the Blue Hills house had been bought with a big loan, a loan they likely thought Sree and I would help repay. Appa and Amma were proud nonetheless.

When Appa was proud or unsure about being proud, he talked about his childhood. We all knew he had grown up in the city, not some village in the outlands, and that his family, while fiscally challenged, didn't live below the poverty line or anything like that. But when Appa told these stories, he tended to exaggerate the difficulties of his starting point. He was practically a slumdog millionaire.

I often got the sense that he believed Sree and I, and a lot of people really, were insufficiently impressed with what he'd achieved.

Sometimes, he'd say, 'Wait till you become older. There's no ladder, you'll see.'

Amma had a similar refrain about the difficulties of running a family. These usually came in one-word form, attached to a sigh. 'Compromise,' she'd say, for instance. Or 'Sacrifice'. Or 'Life'. Sree and I used to make fun of her by saying random words in the tone she used. 'GlobalWarming,' he'd say, sighing. 'JosephStalin,' I'd say, sighing even more deeply.

10

For Appa, meanwhile, the Civic had become a problem. Shortly after Sree left, Appa had sneaked to the porch and covered the car with its silver protective sheet. I saw him watching it from the window whenever I visited his room.

To him, I suppose, the car represented a kind of foolish miscalculation and overconfidence in the future. Maybe he imagined people looking at our house and whispering, *Such a pity*.

That Saturday, Appa came home with several bottles clanging in a black plastic bag. I was the one who opened the door. By then our siege had dissolved and we were once again shifting states.

'What's in the bag?' I asked. I knew the answer already.

'Whisky,' Appa confirmed.

I tried not to look alarmed. In fact, seeing that Appa was expecting a reaction, I downplayed mine even more, letting him pass without further questions.

This must have annoyed him because he shouted, 'Why should I be the only one who lives the way he's supposed to?'

Amma came out of the living room and went to the kitchen.

'All my life,' Appa continued, 'I have worked hard to be a good husband and a good father. Every night, people have invited me for drinks. Every. Single. Night. And do you know what I've said? I have said no, I have to get home. What was the point? Why should I be the only one following the rules?'

Just the act of holding these bottles seemed to make Appa drunk. But the whole thing ended there. He left them on the kitchen counter, where they remained a dumb prop. Later it turned out that he hadn't even bought the liquor himself. A customer had forgotten it in the changing room.

The following day, Amma had me visit Appa at the shop to drop off his lunch.

Royal Textiles had two outlets in Trivandrum, down from three, after our Ernakulam branch had closed. It wasn't a big business by any stretch of the imagination, but it had been around for a while and I liked to think the name had some local stature. The outlet I stopped by was a squat building with two small floors and a glass front. A mannequin stood looking out. Sreenath used to say that her name was Veronica. She and Appa were in a complicated relationship, hoping one day to assimilate into mainstream society.

Inside, Appa was dealing with a customer, the sort that made you pull out entire shelves only to find nothing impressive. The high-intensity tube light sheened off Appa's thick oily hair. He kept sipping warm water from my old Thermos.

We all knew Appa was his happiest when serving customers, even the annoying ones. Customers liked him too. He was handsome and good with small talk. His movements were confident. That day, however, Appa looked puffed up, explosive. One of the other staff members volunteered to take over. Appa refused and went on pulling clothes from the shelves like he was disembowelling them.

He ignored my presence, and anyway I had nothing to tell him. I sat in a corner for a few minutes listening to music. The cleaning woman brought me a glass of molten tea. Finally, Appa said, 'Nothing better to do, as usual. There he is. Writing poems in the air.'

I slammed the glass down and walked out of the shop.

A long time ago, around eleventh grade, Father Vice-Principal

Pauli had summoned Appa to his cabin and said, 'Your son has the heart of a poet.'

I was in the cabin too. Appa glared at me. 'We'll fix it, Father.'

Father Pauli laid out the poems he'd confiscated from my desk. One was about seeing the maths teacher's waist through her saree. But it was so abstract, Father had interpreted it as a rumination on dawn.

He said, 'It doesn't have to be a bad thing these days. Have you heard of Piyush Pandey?'

'The actor?'

'Who? No. Piyush Pandey is the National Creative Director of Ogilvy and Mather. Know Ogilvy and Mather?'

'The cigarette company.'

'Advertising agency. Very widely respected. Pablo Neruda. Octavio Paz. Paulo Coelho. Gabriel García Márquez.'

'Yes?'

'They are all very well-respected writers. So it doesn't have to be a bad thing. We don't even have to look that far. Malayattoor Ramakrishnan IAS. M. T. Vasudevan Nair. O. V. Vijayan? All held in high respect.'

He kept using the word 'respect'. Appa cared for the Church much more than he cared for temples or Hindu priests. Father Pauli told him that Piyush Pandey was a good friend of his – they'd studied together at St Stephen's – and that he would get me an internship at the end of school if my grades were consistent. By then I had just joined the humanities stream much to Sree's grudging disbelief and Appa's disappointed acceptance.

Father died a year later. Worse, he died on vacation, frivolously scootering along a sunny Goa beach. Appa took it personally. Around then he started calling me 'The Poet' and never stopped.

While I wanted to do something in arts, the last poem I'd written was some six years back.

At home, I told Amma, 'Next time he forgets lunch, you go feed him yourself.'

*

That was the week Appa closed the joint bank account he shared with Sreenath, withdrawing all the money in it. To be clear, the job that Sree had was part of his course, a bit like a compulsory internship. He did get a stipend but that went to a different account and was virtually nothing. The joint one was where Appa transferred money for monthly expenses.

After dealing with the bank, Appa called Sreenath's CA institute, telling them he wasn't going to pay tuition for the coming semester and that he wanted to be removed from their list of guardians.

The institute wouldn't have known what to make of Appa's request, and would have contacted Sree to get more information. Sree would also have received a text message about his bank account. I hoped Appa was doing all of this to get a reaction out of him – in fact, I sensed Appa softening somewhat after he dealt each blow – but to Sreenath, it must have made his expulsion seem final.

When all this was happening, I visited him a couple of times. Sree was subsisting mostly on coffee, Cheetos, instant noodles and cheap takeaway. He'd stopped going to the institute and to his articleship.

One time Sreenath seemed to have been asleep when I rang the doorbell, and remained dazed, maybe hungover, as he let me in. Joel was there too, sleeping shirtless on the dining table. Looked like a body about to undergo post-mortem.

The house itself wasn't much worse than before. Garbage accumulated in a large plastic bag. The mattress had been dragged to the edge of the living-room floor, by the window. A couple of notebooks lay on top of it, in a bright patch of sun.

Sree was mad when it came to keeping notebooks. He had a stack that was nearly into the hundreds. He sourced them cheap; you could tell that from how oily the paper was. As far as I'd seen, these notebooks were filled with random business ideas or his daily schedule or his coursework. He wrote everything down using pens of different colours. Some sections were elaborately highlighted. Some had sheets of paper stapled to them.

Once, a few years back, Sree had accidentally left a notebook inside the fridge and I'd glimpsed in it a paragraph that resembled a journal entry: *It's only a matter of effort. If you put effort into it, anything is possible. Also, past failures don't mean squat. It certainly isn't evidence against yourself. Remember that, for God sakes. You got this.*

What 'this' referred to, I never found out. But reading that paragraph had made me supremely happy and, on behalf of Sree, supremely embarrassed. At home he was always trying to act so invulnerable. I'd stood smirking into the fridge until Amma said, 'If we could afford an AC, we'd get one. Close the door.'

A couple of days later, when Sree was making fun of me for something, I said, 'Look, my past failures don't mean squat. You have to remember that.'

'What did you say?'

'Nothing.'

Sreenath was wearing boxers now and a grey-blue shirt from his year in the Cadet Corps.

I swept my hand across the room and said, 'Sree. Enough. Let's talk it out.'

This was when he told me about his initial reaction to the video, rubbing his eyes and speaking softly.

'You know that habit you had as a kid?' he said.

I knew what he was referring to because he often joked about it.

As a child, when I broke a vase or spilled something on the floor, I would punish myself before Appa or Amma had a chance to scold me. Usually this involved climbing to a high place and jumping off, or hitting myself hard with whatever I could find. Sreenath had a theory that this had left me brain-damaged.

'Right after I saw the video,' Sree said, 'I thought I could cut my wrist a little and go show it downstairs. I was *this* close to doing it, I even googled which way to cut. I still can't believe it.'

Admittedly, a part of me thought: That would have been a good plan, actually. A very strategic move.

'Why are you telling me this now?' I asked.

'Not sure. I was just thinking: Look what you almost did. And for what?'

He got up to wash his face, then began doing push-ups on the floor. Sree used to jog, but he wasn't exactly a model for upper-body strength.

'Is this the start of your revenge saga?'

'Need the endorphins,' he said.

The next time I went over, Sree and Joel were playing Counter-Strike on their laptops. I sat in a corner with my phone and watched football compilations.

At some point I heard Sree joking to Joel that the house was haunted.

'I can feel this vague presence out of the corner of my eyes,' he said. 'Just out of my reach.'

Joel said, 'If there's a rat, we are guaranteed rabies.'

When he went to the kitchen, I asked Sree, 'Do you think this haunting feeling could be a side effect of the video? Because of the voyeur and all that?'

Truth was, nobody seemed to care about the person who'd filmed the video: he was just another guy in public, doing what he wanted. I imagined he looked like our high-school lab tech. Young wiry man with a light moustache. Always smelling his fingers. He was fired for stealing specimens. A kidney here. A toad there. Apparently, they'd found them in his kitchen next to the salt and pepper, still in their jars of formaldehyde.

'What?' Sree said.

'This someone-watching-you-haunting phenomenon. Do you think it's because you were filmed like that?'

'Fuck your pop psychology.'

'Whatever it is, you're clearly bothered,' I said. 'We'll sneak you home and plan out the rest from there. Haven't you made your point?'

'And what point is that?'

'Look, if you're worried about facing Appa and Amma –'

This seemed to make him angry.

'I'm good. Thank you for your service, middleman.'

The 'middleman' stuff got on my nerves and I left a short while later.

The time after that, Dhruti, Meghna and Arjun Samurai were at Sree's place, but Sree himself wasn't. He'd gone to meet Anita near her house. She was supposed to come over but her parents had wanted her to stay and talk to some guests.

I asked Dhruti if everything was all right.

'So far, so good,' she said.

She was sitting on the floor next to Arjun, filling out a sheaf of yellow forms: 'Some extension stuff for Anita. She couldn't come to the university today and get the applications.' Dhruti grinned at me. 'You want to do it?'

'My handwriting is hieroglyphics,' I said.

Arjun said to Dhruti, 'If Elsie were here, she'd be all, "Is admitting to bad handwriting just a masculinity thing? Is it? Is it?"'

I had no idea who Elsie was.

'Is it? Is it?' Dhruti said, not looking up from the forms.

Before I'd interrupted them, Dhruti and Arjun had been sitting way too close and talking about the video. The cosiness, at my family's expense, really annoyed me.

Presumably launching now from the topic of Sree's situation, Arjun said, 'Standing up for what you believe is impressive either way. Failure to do that is the cause of everything happening in our country today, starting with the current government. I mean, you know that guy, Madhu BR or whatever his name is, he apparently broke up with his girlfriend because his family had some issue with her caste.'

Dhruti said, 'He was on Twitter the other day saying something ardently anti-BJP.' She started laughing. 'He tagged Arundhati Roy.'

'These are the guys they should really cancel.'

'I mean, cancel them all, but I get your point.'

I said, 'Yeah, that's some major bullshit. I was reading this book about casteism by Sujatha Gidla sometime back. Have you read it?'

'I saw the reviews.' Arjun groped his hair-bun with one hand and, with the other, offered me a cigarette. I felt everyone was smoking way more than they normally would have. I accepted anyway. He continued, 'And for sure, man, major bullshit. This guy is an embodiment of idiocy. I mean, the balls, really. It's something.'

'Incredible stuff.'

I sat down and, despite my earlier annoyance, felt slightly calm. Dhruti and Arjun went on talking. First about *Ratatouille*, then an episode of *MasterChef*, then a cartoon Anita had made. It was about brands exploiting the epithet 'superwoman'. She'd posted it a couple of nights back. One comment on the post said: *Tried reaching out. Are you okay?*

I was surprised to see her online at all.

Meghna, who'd been in the kitchen, came out and hovered.

'The knob was fine before,' she said. 'It looks fried now.'

'Spoken like a true landlord,' Dhruti said. Arjun approved.

'So is Anita a hundred per cent not coming?' Meghna asked.

'Looks unlikely.'

'I keep calling her to ask if she's okay.'

'Don't do it too often. She doesn't like it. Looks disaster-touristy.'

'Did she say that?'

Meanwhile I was thinking about having to return home soon, and about the way Appa had stayed by the window staring at the car.

I almost said: My family is insane.

11

For some time then, the idea of going to the police had been making rounds at home. I'd told Appa that Sree and Anita had tried this themselves – there had also been vague talk of an online complaint – though Appa didn't believe a casual approach would come to anything. There was no FIR, no case number, no real clue if it was even being looked at. But having said all this, Appa would also say he didn't care enough to do anything about it – just like he said he didn't care enough about future plans or the issues that might be posed by Anita's family.

I suppose there was *some* positive development: Sree, by himself, had managed to get a copy of the video removed, even if only a couple of days later, he'd found another one on a different site. When I asked him about it, he was dismissive. 'If people want to watch it so much, let them. It's not the end of the world.' Other than that, he didn't seem the least interested in discussion. By then I was taking a few passes too, though for the most part, I was pessimistic about the odds and my efforts were tame.

It was Amma who convinced Appa to go to the police. If the video was taken down before more people saw it, especially our relatives, we could at least maintain some deniability, even when word got around.

It was Wednesday noon. Once Appa said he'd do it, he paced around the living room, rubbing his temples and picking his way through a whole bag of salted peanuts. After that he sped up. Maybe he was afraid his confidence would run out if he waited too long. Appa trimmed his moustache, found his best formal shirt and trousers, and put on the costly watch he saved for weddings. He asked me to go with him since I was the one who knew the technical details. A while later, we were inside the Civic, strapping our seat belts in. The car still smelled of soft plastic and sticky leather. Appa had brought the thick blue folder that held all our birth certificates, identity cards and medical records. He placed it on the backseat and started the car. The day was bright, made even brighter by the clear windscreen.

Appa drove around for a long time. We must have passed several police stations along the way. Each time we scrolled past one, he slowed down, had a brief look, then accelerated once again.

Based on where we stopped in the end, Appa's target must have been a police station that was far enough that we wouldn't run into anyone we knew; skeletal enough that it wouldn't be too embarrassing or overwhelming; and not at all crowded, so we wouldn't be kept waiting.

In retrospect, using these selection criteria was a mistake. We should have gone to one of those busier police stations where officers clicked their heels together and were too occupied to take a personal interest in anything.

This station was provincial and resembled a run-down house. We'd driven around so much, I wasn't even sure where we were any more. Appa pulled into the gravel compound, cut the engine and sat in his seat for a long time – too long, apparently, because a police constable knocked on the windscreen and said, 'This is not a cinema theatre. Do you need anything?' Already we were off to a bad start.

Appa got out with the blue folder, apologised and patted his pockets for nothing. The constable was on his way out, so Appa stood around for a while longer. This time, he pretended to check his phone. Only when I asked him if everything was okay did he finally make a move towards the building.

The old-house aesthetic continued inside as well. Its peeling walls were joined together at the corners by intricate cobwebs. The furniture was from another century; a gramophone wouldn't have looked out of place. Symbolically speaking, all bad.

A police officer was sitting at his desk reading the newspaper.

'Can I speak to the Station House Officer?' Appa asked.

We hadn't even started but I could already feel his embarrassment.

'What do you need?' the officer asked.

'I have a complaint I'd like to file.'

He told us to take a seat, put the paper away and pulled out a white register from the drawer. He scribbled something in it and asked, 'What's the complaint?'

Appa replied with a line he must have rehearsed beforehand. 'It's a cybercrime,' he said. 'There's a video of my son with a girl. It's on the internet. We don't know who put it there. It's a bad kind of video. We'd like to get it removed.'

Without taking his eyes off the register, the officer got up, told us to wait, and went into the backroom. Ten or fifteen minutes later, a thinner, moustachioed officer, who looked only a few years older than me, came out and sat down. I don't know if the sound of someone sitting down can convey annoyance, but it definitely felt like that with this guy. He cracked his knuckles and went through the register again. His name-tag said 'Arun'. Unlike the previous officer, Arun was fit, his uniform was ironed and his shoes were mirrors.

'You have a cybercrime to report?' he asked. He reminded me of an SS officer I'd seen in my history textbook a long time ago – or maybe this is a resemblance I have superimposed on him after the fact.

'Yes, sir,' Appa said.

'And?'

Appa repeated his dialogue: 'There's a video of my son with a girl. It's on the internet. We don't know who put it there. It's a bad kind of video. We'd like to –'

'What do you mean *a bad kind of video*?'

Appa hesitated, so he asked, 'Pornographic kind?'

68

'Yes, sir.'

'So say that. Let's be clear here.'

'Yes, sir.'

I wished Appa would stop addressing him as 'sir'. It wasn't just the difference in age that bothered me – this guy was clearly feeding off it. In the meantime, Appa had grown smaller. His shoulders drooped. The watch on his wrist looked like it might slide off. There was such an incongruity between his fancy clothes and his demeanour that it made him look even more powerless, as though someone else had bathed him and dressed him up. You could have packed him into a suitcase.

The officer pointed at me. 'This here is your famous son?'

'My older son is the one in the video, sir.'

'But you haven't brought him.'

Appa shook his head.

The officer sighed and leaned back in his chair.

For the next few minutes, he asked us all sorts of questions, starting with the relationship between Sreenath and Anita. Even when I was the one answering them, he kept his eyes locked on Appa.

From the topic of Sree's relationship, he began meandering. He asked Appa what he did for a living, whether Amma had a job, how old they each were, where exactly we lived, and even what kind of money we made every month. I thought the fact that I was an almost-journalist might temper him, but nothing doing.

At one point I tried to bring him on track by asking, 'Is it possible to get the videos removed soon?'

He stared at me for a few seconds, then ignored me. To emphasise his right to ask whatever he wanted, he invented a few more strange questions. Appa tried to set himself apart by answering everything with extra enthusiasm.

Finally, the officer passed a piece of paper towards us and said, 'Links. Write them down.'

I had bookmarked the ones I knew of and had tried calling Sree for more information before leaving home. He hadn't answered. Appa had said, 'Let him do what he wants at his end. What we are doing, we are doing for us.'

I began copying the links on to the paper. Halfway through, the officer pulled it back towards him, stared at it and sighed. He must have sighed at least twenty times while we were there.

The computer on his desk was consistent with the rest of the place in that it was a cashew-white model that used to populate computer labs when I was in middle school. Once it opened with the tired Windows chime, he entered a link from the paper, waited for the video to buffer, and played it.

'Any idea who might have filmed this?' he asked.

'No, don't think so,' I said.

He turned the volume all the way up, but aside from rustling and unclear mumbling, there was barely any audio in the first place.

I could sense Appa squirming next to me. The position of the desk was such that other people had to pass behind it to cross from one room to the other. There weren't a lot of officers at the station, but it certainly caught the attention of those who *were* there. One of them joked as he walked by, saying, 'Arun, at least wait till you get home, man.'

The officer frowned and extended his palm towards us. 'Look what I have to deal with': that's what he seemed to say.

Soon, a young peon was standing behind the computer squinting at the screen, thoroughly entertained by the free show. The whole thing was making me uncomfortable and indignant, and I tried to convey this through a series of Morse throat-clearings and seat-shuffles. The officer turned around, looked at the peon, and looked back at the screen again. Keeping his eyes there, he said to Appa, 'You people have no problem doing all this in public, but this now is an issue? The audacity.' He looked at the peon and repeated, 'The audacity, you know? Right out there in public. Can you believe it? Couldn't even wait to get a room.'

I wanted to point out that his remark about getting a room was ironic. I'm no expert, but till a few years back at least, the police were rumoured to frequently raid hotels looking for prostitution rackets. In the process, they'd drag out innocent couples and make them call their homes and summon their parents to secure their release. Even though this had nothing to do with Sreenath's case, not really – in fact, they'd rented hotel rooms a bunch of times – I'd recently used this point to help rationalise his side of things with Appa and Amma.

I'm okay at pushing back but avoid it if possible. Now I was not only embarrassed by our treatment, but also feeling responsible for protecting Appa.

In the end, I said, 'There's nothing to be gained by discussing what's already happened, sir. We just want to move forward.'

Not the best response. I hadn't been to the police before, not even during my internship, but I had been to government offices – to get my driving licence or pay land tax, for instance – and the best course, I felt, was to follow the invisible script and get it over with, whatever that involved. In most cases, deviation from this betrayed not bravery, but naivety and a willingness to waste your own time.

The officer turned towards me and sat back in his chair.

'What's that again?' he asked.

This just about loosened my sphincter. I could have laid an egg. Next to me, I felt Appa glaring. The peon walked away with his tray of glasses.

'It's just a complicated situation, sir,' I said. 'We'd appreciate it if you could help us deal with it in the best way possible.'

The officer turned to Appa. 'You realise what you have done, right?'

Appa said yes even though I was pretty sure he had no idea what the officer was referring to. Right then, you could have got him to admit to anything. Did he smuggle drugs? Yes. Did he assassinate Kennedy? Sure. Was he in cahoots with Judas? Indeed.

The officer went on. 'Your son has practically destroyed this young woman's life. Do you understand that?'

Appa nodded. Again I didn't keep my mouth shut.

'Sir,' I said, picturing Anita, 'the young woman in question is more than fine and perfectly capable of handling the situation.'

'Mind your tone,' the officer snapped.

Back to Appa: 'I can't even imagine what this woman must be

going through now. You have practically ruined her future. Can she show her face anywhere? Can she get a good job? Will anyone treat her with respect?'

I got the sense that this officer was the sort of person who fantasised about rescuing women from the verge of being assaulted. The women would then fall in love with him and owe him for the rest of their lives.

'We just want to get the video removed, sir,' Appa said. He was pleading.

'Easy for you to say. Get the video removed. Do you think the internet is like my fridge? That I can put things in and take them out whenever I please. It's not so easy, understand that first. Once something like this gets posted online, it becomes very, very hard to remove it.'

Before I could respond, Appa turned to me and asked me to go outside. I hesitated; then, seeing that the officer was waiting for me to leave as well, got up and walked to the car. There, I leaned against the door, running through the list of laws I had looked up earlier – Section 66E, 67A, all that – and wishing I had said something snappier or at least more informed, if I had to say anything at all.

Appa came out much sooner than expected. He got in the car and started the engine. My impression was if I had stayed outside, he would have driven away without noticing.

On our way back, everything looked grey and hostile. Appa sat close to the steering wheel. He didn't talk. I asked him what had happened at the station but he continued ignoring me.

We were stopped at a red light when he asked for Sreenath's address.

'Why do you want to know?'

'I need to see him.'

'About what happened at the station?'

'Yes.'

'You're going to shout at him, Appa.'

He didn't say anything. The traffic light in front of us was counting down. It had reached twenty-five.

'Are you going to shout?'

'I just need to see him.'

'Tell me you won't shout.'

It felt like a chance to get them talking.

'Appa?'

'Tell me if you know it, otherwise forget it.'

I gave Appa the directions then realised even before we got there that I had made a mistake. Appa's anger started bubbling. A biker overtook us on the wrong side and he nearly started a fight. With that now-boiled brain of his, Appa decided to go flat out, almost slicing the car on a black-and-white divider.

When we got to Sreenath's lane, I refused to tell him the house number. It wasn't a big lane – maybe ten houses – but there was no way he could try all the doors.

What Appa did instead was park in the middle of the road and press down on the horn.

'I'm not stopping till you tell me where he lives.'

A man opened his balcony door and started shouting at us for waking him up so early. It was late afternoon, but he didn't seem to care.

One minute later, I saw the curtains move in Sreenath's house. He appeared at his door, wearing just his boxers.

Appa saw him in the rear-view mirror. He opened his door and stepped outside. For a few seconds, he seemed unsure about what to do. Then he reached for the blue folder on the backseat and took out Sree's birth certificate and other important documents.

'Appa, come on.' I got out of the car as he walked towards Sreenath's house.

Sreenath looked ready to run back inside. Appa dumped the files by the gate, then returned to the car.

This time I didn't get in. Sure enough, Appa didn't ask.

Once Appa drove away, Sree left his doorstep, picked up his documents and closed the door before I could talk to him.

I took an auto home without trying.

Later, I found out from Amma that the officer had told Appa to come back with Sree. Or better yet, to go to another station that was more equipped to handle cybercrimes. I think he also threatened the possibility of public obscenity charges. Appa was vague about the exact words the officer had used – and I suspect that a failed bribery had transpired – but it was clear that he was tired, no longer interested in pursuing the matter.

12

Anita's parents continued to remain blissfully unaware of the situation. Meanwhile I slept poorly. Every time I left home, I returned with chocolates and banana chips. I kept them in my room and gained about three kilos in two weeks. I suppose the junk food also worked as a form of protest. Often I didn't eat meals at home – not with Appa and Amma at least. Their quarrelling had escalated since our visit to the police station. Appa had now suffered more humiliation than Amma which seemed to give him the right to be angrier than her.

Everything sent him over the top: a delayed delivery of stock at the warehouse; the steam iron taking too long to heat up; a leaking pipe which Amma, once upon a time, had assured him was working fine.

'You need me to do everything,' Appa said. 'You can't even be bothered to call the plumber. You can't even handle this one simple thing on your own.'

For the most part, Amma kept quiet and went about her day. This wasn't because she was incapable of retorting. Rather, she knew she could inflict maximum damage by making Appa feel guilty and ashamed of the things he would end up saying.

When the scene was at its most intense, I recorded a voice clip of the chaos and sent it to Sreenath.

He'd been ignoring my laments about the police and ignored this too for a day, before finally replying: *You're an asshole*.

An hour later I told him to go fist himself.

That same evening, Appa came home with a 55-inch Chinese TV, acting busy as the men from the shop nailed it to the wall, took our old one and fled. Appa said he'd got the TV cheap from a friend and that the offer was only available for a short time. I thought everyone was losing their minds.

'Help me figure it out, will you?' Appa said.

The blue home screen quickly filled with Chinese characters.

'Figure it out yourself,' I said.

Aside from a few visits to Sree's place and other random outings, I didn't mingle much with anyone. I searched for jobs abroad. Frankfurt, Seattle, Montreal. It didn't matter where, as long as the place was far away. When the job thing started to seem impossible – which happened fast – I began looking for courses abroad and even mailed a university in Paris about a journalism scholarship. The French never wrote back, realising no doubt that I wasn't a desirable import.

The internship was still happening on the side, but I'd lost interest. One evening, just after the video came to light, I botched a story about a flower show and angered the organiser, a real mafioso type. From then on, I barely got any assignments and stopped visiting the office even for occasional check-ins.

Instead, I was spending time in the public library reading Malayalam translations of Russian classics or hanging around one of the city's art centres where they hosted small events. Some of these featured directors or writers who had a niche following. I imagined asking them to come to my house and having them talk to Appa and Amma. If they could provide a larger perspective, perhaps some kind of a peace agreement could be brokered.

Once, thinking I was on an assignment, somebody at the Samskrithi Bhavan let me talk to a young film-maker from Cardiff. After a while, he started asking me questions. That's when I really let it rip – telling him first about the paper I interned for, then about my plan to go abroad, and finally about the video issue. I must have said all this in a sardonic and light-hearted way because his response was equally flippant.

'Have you heard of *The Jeremy Kyle Show*?' he asked.

I googled that at home, watched five minutes of sparking, bickering families, and then couldn't get it out of my head again.

I also had a weird impulse that involved Dhruti. I'd been looking at her Instagram photos for a while; some with her friends, including older ones featuring Sree and Anita; some with her family and her house. Her post on Valentine's Day implied she was single. One recent picture showed her and her mother play-fighting for a hammock. Next to them is an interrupted breakfast. Orange Tropicana, bull's-eyes with bright yolks, breadcrumbs on the scratchy wooden table. They are on a balcony in the stratosphere. Her mother is grinning. Below, the city looks level.

All of a sudden I wanted very much to spend time with Dhruti. I'd been meaning to talk to her about her police friend anyway, so I had reason enough to ask for a quick coffee. She agreed to meet me at a cafe near her apartment.

It was early in the evening and school buses were clogging up traffic, shedding children everywhere. We chose tables outside and Dhruti kept fanning herself with the menu. Her shampoo had a fruit scent – peach or pineapple, mixed with something more complicated.

'I've been swimming,' she said. 'Well, stewing in a pool, more like. I'm always in a pool when it's summer.'

The discussion about the police took ten minutes. She asked about my parents. I changed the subject. She told me about hers. They were dentists. Both of them? Yes, that's how they'd met. That's why she had such inhumanly proper teeth. Dhruti put her fingers in her mouth and grinned to show me.

'I get why you don't want to talk about all that, though,' she said. 'I mean, mine can often be –' she scanned the tablecloth for a word '– tyrannical. Oppressive?'

Maybe I didn't look convinced. Not that I needed to be, by any means. But she seemed on the verge of launching an anecdote. I changed the subject again.

Dhruti was wearing a T-shirt that said 'Anime Club'. We talked about *Naruto*, *Cowboy Bebop* and the plane scene from *Ghost in the Shell*.

I tried out a story about how Sree and I used to play Pokémon as kids. Inevitably he would be the trainer and I would be the Pokémon. He'd go 'bite' or 'tackle' or 'scratch', and I'd do it to whoever was standing in front of me.

'Hilarious,' Dhruti said, sipping her lime soda.

She then told me she was bingeing Satyajit Ray's entire filmography.

'I can't resist a good Bengali film. Especially the old stuff.'

I said, 'For us Malayalis, I think Bengalis are the only *real* intellectual kin in all of India.'

What a pompous thing to say, but thankfully she agreed. In fact, 'My father is actually from West Bengal,' Dhruti said. 'Calcutta.'

'I figured there was something. Your name isn't one of the typical Kerala ones.' In the same breath I also added, 'Plus you're way too good-looking to be a full Malayali.'

'C'mon, Malayalis are good-looking.'

The traffic and the school children were now clearing up. A passing cloud cast some cool on our side of the street. Those thirty–forty minutes went by fast. Nothing much happened. But when I got home, I felt an enormous and enormously disproportionate sense of relief. Like I had other places to be now.

Later I texted Sreenath to say I'd met Dhruti about some FIR stuff.

What the fuck, he said. Then nothing.

That night I modelled shirtless in front of the mirror and tried a breaststroke. I wondered if I had the features of a good-looking Malayali.

13

Two visits I made to Sree's place stood out. Anita was present both times. On the first occasion, a bald muscular guy opened the door and let me in. Sree was sitting on the living-room floor. Opposite him was a very tall woman, her hair done in pigtails. Anita was on the cracked plastic chair. They were all talking over each other and laughing in a casual way. This stopped as soon as I made my appearance.

The room was dim, lit only by a single low-watt bulb. Someone had arranged empty bottles of diet soda into bowling pins. A window had been opened. It gave the air a wet, sulky weight. The bald guy sat down next to Sreenath and glanced at his watch.

Unlike Sree's usual company, these visitors were slightly older, maybe in their mid-twenties. The woman seemed familiar, but I couldn't figure out how. All of them were sipping beer and eating fried anchovies out of a leaf parcel.

'Hey,' I said.

'Hey,' Anita said. 'Everything good?'

'Yeah. Just wanted to drop by.'

Sreenath didn't look my way. There was a blunt animosity between us now. I was angry with him because of the humiliation we'd suffered at the police station. He was angry with me for going there in the first place and also for telling Appa his address.

I excused myself and used the bathroom. When I returned, the woman was hugging Sree and Anita, saying how great it had been to catch up again. The guy shook their hands and grabbed his bag. It was cluttered with enamel pins and buttons including one that said 'F#@% the Teletubbies'.

A few minutes later, as Anita herself was leaving, I asked her who the visitors were. Sreenath was inside, looking for her phone charger.

'Just people we know,' Anita said. She was in an oversized black hoodie even though it was about 35°C.

'From university? I feel like I have seen the woman before.'

'They are in a band, so you might have seen them perform. She is the singer. The guy plays bass. There are three others.'

As soon as Anita said it, I was able to place the woman. I had seen her band's posters on Facebook and Instagram. Formed in Trivandrum, based everywhere. Soft rock. Not too new and not that big.

I figured they were friends checking in – Sree and Anita seemed to be getting a lot of those.

The other visit that stood out was two weeks after the police-station trip.

It was a cloudy evening and I'd been playing football with some school friends when lightning struck near the field. As excited as I was by the added danger and the possibility of my problems vaporising, everyone else decided to pack up. I rode over to Sree's.

No sooner had I arrived than he announced his plans to go grocery shopping. Anita, who was carrying a waste bin to the kitchen, told him she would tag along. She needed to get gum.

It was clear Sree didn't want me to go with them and entirely possible that they were lying about groceries so I would leave. I didn't really care. I wanted to wander around as much as possible before returning home.

'I need to get a few things as well,' I said.

Sree didn't object and only said, 'Cool.'

It was dark and windy outside, and I could really smell the

nearby sewer. Since we were walking through empty back alleys, we spread out and took up the entire road. All three of us smoked silently until Sreenath got a phone call and fell behind. I turned to Anita and asked, 'Are they expecting you home soon?'

'They are,' she said. 'I'm running late.'

Anita checked her watch and sped up. She was still wearing the black hoodie. I'd decided this was because the video was making her feel self-conscious about her body, but who knows, maybe she just liked the hoodie.

'Must be tough, all this.'

'Sorry?'

'All this,' I said, gesturing to the road and to us walking, as if I meant that. 'Must be kind of tough, right?'

'Certainly very strange,' Anita said.

'Right. True. I don't think I'd have coped.'

'Que será será.'

'You aren't worried about home?'

Anita didn't say anything for a while. Then: 'Maybe I'll tell them on my own after all.'

'Do they suspect something?'

'I have been a little sick all month. They think I ate something horrible. Bad fish. Cthulhu, maybe. I don't know.'

'Is it anxiety?'

She didn't reply. We turned into a narrow lane and became a single file. Anita in front, me second.

'They aren't violent people, are they?' I asked.

'My parents? Haven't been so far but there's a first time for everything. Do you miss your brother?'

'I miss peace and stability.'

'Right.'

'How did you guys get together anyway? He never tells me anything.'

To be honest, I don't know what I was digging for here. Only that I didn't want to waste Anita's admission about being sick and possibly anxious.

She hesitated once again before saying, 'Back in the second

year of undergrad, your brother tried to start this association. For *creative endeavours*. It was very stupid. Nobody there was interested in that kind of thing. I turned out to be the only other member. So yeah, a two-person club.'

I was so sure they'd met while bitching about home at the water cooler.

'Very meet-cute.'

'Thanks, I guess?'

'Sree told me you used to quiz.'

'Bournvita had a camp at school.'

'Did your parents put you up to it?'

'I just liked reading those guides.'

'Distraction from all the noise at home. Bury yourself in a thick book.'

'I think I just liked reading them.'

'Know the capital of Iceland?'

'Reykjavik. Are you kidding me?'

'But can you spell it.'

'Y before k, j after it, no c at the end.'

'I really like your art stuff as well.'

'Thanks.'

We took another turn into a wider main road. Neon signs of jewellery shops floated upside down in puddles. The air smelled of strong filter coffee.

'Sree told me once that, as a kid, you wanted to be abducted.'

'What?'

'By aliens, not paedophiles.'

'I still wouldn't mind getting abducted by aliens,' Anita said. She looked straight up. 'In fact, what I wouldn't give.'

The supermarket we went to was one of the biggest in the city, though that in itself isn't saying much. While Anita and Sreenath walked through the aisles, I trailed behind them feeling jealous about how easy they were together and how especially familial they looked here, surrounded by curry powders and dishwashing liquids.

It was at the frozen section that we ran into a bunch of their old juniors. Four guys.

The undergrad university that Anita and Sreenath had attended wasn't really what you would call Ivy League. It was known for giving students a good technical foundation, sure, but culturally speaking, it was in a shambles. Present company and their close friends excluded, it wouldn't have been strange to find the male alumni on crowded buses having impassioned debates on the circumference of women's body parts, or on the streets, starting fights.

I'd actually seen this group out of the corner of my eye as soon as I entered the supermarket. The shortest of the four was wearing his university uniform. He was the most animated of the lot. At one point, I'd caught him with his mouth open, imitating an ecstatic moan, while his friends giggled and scolded him. The expression he was mimicking was one that Sree had worn for most of the video. It made him look like he was about to throw up. Flushing the image from my head had taken me weeks. What the junior had done was near-perfect.

I don't know if Sree and Anita had seen any of this. I suppose they had and decided to ignore it. This seemed to be working too, and I thought we'd lost the group until they reappeared at the frozen section.

For a while, they tried to pass off as regular shoppers while whispering and glancing at us. The short guy seemed to be pushing one of the others in our direction. The pushee resisted, planting his feet firmly on the floor each time and pushing back.

The aisle was small and narrow, so it wasn't like we were standing far away. I asked Sree and Anita if they were done. The group was becoming charged and noisy. Anita turned their way and said, 'Everything okay with you guys? Do you need something?' She'd said it loud enough that two other shoppers, standing in the opposite aisle, paused what they were doing and stared. Her voice had come out wobbly.

The juniors stopped giggling. The short guy finally said, 'No, madam, nothing. Well, actually, Dileep here was wondering if you guys could give us an autograph. You and your boyfriend.'

Dileep, the person who was being pushed, turned to the short guy and hissed at him.

Anita asked if he had a pen.

'What?'

'To sign your autograph. Do you have a pen?'

While the others laughed nervously, this fucker found a pen in his bag and stepped forward, pulling out and spreading the pocket of his white shirt.

I looked at Sreenath to see if he was okay with this. Maybe I shouldn't have been surprised to find that he was as straight-faced as Anita. I, on the other hand, had stiffened and was essentially standing ready to I don't know what. To run? To punch his nose in? To break up a fight?

Once Anita signed the shirt, Sree did as well. He even drew a little heart below his signature and underlined it twice.

'I will always cherish this memory,' the short guy said.

'Glad to help,' Anita said.

We walked to the checkout, paid for two packets of buns, and left the store. Anita mumbled that she didn't need gum anyway.

It had started to drizzle. While Sreenath crossed the road to get cigarettes, Anita and I stood around beside the store. I watched her absent-mindedly peel movie posters from the roadside wall. She was squinting.

'I'm sorry about that,' I said.

Anita continued peeling. 'Meh. It's only embarrassing if you let it be.'

'I guess that's true.'

'Just humans being human. As they always are and always will be.'

'Yup.'

'Anthropology-wise interesting, though.' Her voice was still strained.

'Yeah.'

'It's good material, I suppose.'

'Maybe.'

Not long before that, two of my classmates – ones who'd been to my house and met Sreenath – had asked me about the video, having come to know of it from two separate sources. I figured its local viewership must have been increasing every day. It was possible, even likely, that someone had turned it into a WhatsApp forward and that it was circulating in various sleazy groups.

News like this spread pretty fast in Trivandrum; I guess that's the case with most sex scandals. A few such videos, or related online threads, had comments asking about the status of the couple. Theories often involved murder or suicide. If the video was around long enough, it mushroomed a subculture of its own, some with urban legends surrounding them. In high school, I remember there being one that people used to watch at sleepovers. Rumour was, if you played it in a dark room, between 2:33 and 2:43 a.m., the girl in the video would appear before you and cut off your prick to take revenge. Some seniors had even added a chant: 'Manifest yourself, woman, and take the virgin you most desire.'

I'm not saying *this* video had achieved that level of popularity by then, but the fact that Sree was in his uniform must have given it an ideal circle to grow within and pushed it towards a head-start. I'm sure it didn't help that Anita was pretty.

When Sreenath returned, the two of them lit cigarettes. I lit one in solidarity. Sree produced a half-laugh and shook his head like he couldn't believe what had just happened.

Before we could walk back to the house, the group of juniors emerged from the store, still making a lot of noise. The short guy shouted, 'Do you people want to get something to drink? It's on us.'

'Man, fuck these morons,' I said. 'I can call a couple of my football friends. Five minutes it'll take. These guys will need dental surgery.' This was just anger, something to say. I might also have been trying to impress or console Anita.

Sreenath seemed more embarrassed by my being embarrassed than by the juniors themselves. I'd noticed the same thing in Anita as well.

'Will you relax,' Sree said. 'They are harmless.'

He shouted back: 'Maybe some other time.'

Anita checked her watch. 'I have to head home. I'm beyond late now.'

The junior clapped and held up a victory sign. We left them there and started walking to Sree's place. They were still watching us when I looked back.

III

Cave of Forgotten Dreams

14

Not much changed for a week. Anger: high. Arguments: frequent. Clarity: nil. Then suddenly, on the following Saturday night, a car pulled up outside the house. Appa was watching the new TV, I was tying my shoes, getting ready to go for a jog, and Amma was at the dining table, solving a book of maths puzzles. In retrospect, it's strange that we had the time or the mindset to just sit there. I heard three doors closing, followed by the double-beep of the lock.

Appa went to the curtains and peeked out. The doorbell rang.

'Is it Mathews?' Amma asked. Mathews worked in the shop with Appa. I wanted it to be Mathews too. Mathews, Akhil, Tulsi, Chandru, anybody.

Appa said he didn't know, he couldn't see.

The doorbell rang a second time, then a third. He walked slowly to the hallway. I followed him. Appa opened the door by a fraction.

'Yes?' he said. I could tell he already knew what was coming.

On our doorstep were two men and a woman.

'My name is Mohan,' the older of the two men said. 'I'm the uncle of your son's classmate, Anita. These are Anita's parents. Veena and Ravi. Can we talk? It's important.'

Appa looked like he'd swallowed too much air but was afraid to breathe out. He turned as if to check something behind him, then turned back and opened the door slightly wider. They removed their shoes and walked in. Amma was standing by the dining table, one hand massaging a chair.

To have them here, bodies and everything – so many times I'd imagined this, it was like writing a play and seeing it performed. But Sree was supposed to warn me if this looked probable. His phone had been switched off since the previous afternoon. There was also something odd about the way they came in just like that. You read things in the paper. I'd been worried about some form of roughness right away. Screaming or loud banging. A car through the living-room wall. Punching. Appa or Amma fainting. Until then, my parents' overall stance on the matter had remained: 'We'll cross that bridge when we get there, if we get there.' Privately, I'm sure they must have had more detailed discussions. Since the subject made them even more angry at Sreenath, I only brought it up when I really had to. Perhaps they imagined Anita's parents wouldn't find out after all or that they would keep it to themselves once they did. Now Appa and Amma looked like they were finally on the bridge. It was made of straw and rocking uncontrollably.

Anita's family sat down on the long sofa while Appa sat on the shorter one that formed an L with theirs. He introduced Amma but left me out. I lingered in the hallway.

Anita's mother was a thin woman with obedient bobbed hair. She was wearing a blue kurta that made her seem younger than Amma. She looked smart. Smart as in capable rather than intelligent. Though, I'm sure she's that too. Her husband reminded me of a sad Soviet scientist in exile. Wilting shoulders, thick grey moustache, curly hair, shirt tucked too deep into his trousers.

Mohan was short and balding, and he was the one who spoke first. 'You have another son, yes? Named Sreenath?'

'Yes,' Appa said.

'Is he home?'

'No.'

Mohan nodded, pressed his hands together and asked, 'Do you know?'

Appa thought about this for nearly ten seconds. 'Yes.'

Even before he answered, his pause had had an impact.

Anita's mother moved forward on the sofa, looked directly at Appa, and asked, 'How long have you known, then?'

Appa got that lost expression again and once again he seemed to be considering whether or not to lie. In the end, he uselessly subtracted two weeks and some change. 'About three weeks,' he said.

The room became quiet. Amma, who'd been standing some distance from the sofa, walked over but did not sit down.

'I wish you had shown us some basic courtesy,' Anita's mother said. 'You could have phoned us. You could have come to our house. Anything. It would have been basic courtesy to let us know. It would have helped a lot. A lot.'

Anita's father interlocked his fingers and mumbled something in agreement.

Appa stared at his feet.

'So you have known about this for three weeks,' Anita's mother said. 'Do you know when we found out? Yesterday morning. From a family friend who told a relative.'

She paused and looked from Appa to Amma. 'Anita wouldn't tell us anything. Her friends wouldn't tell us anything. She's been in hiding since yesterday. Her friends say she's fine, but they won't tell us where. They wouldn't even tell us how to reach you. We had to look at the video and look through Anita's university magazine to find your son's face. Can you imagine that? Then today we went to the wrong person's house.'

Anita's mother shook her head like she was too annoyed to explain this.

Mohan said, 'On the class photo, the magazine, it seems, had mixed your son's name with the name of the fellow standing next to him. We thought your son was called something else, so we ended up at the wrong house.'

'We told them nearly everything before the boy was called down,' Anita's mother said. 'Can you imagine the humiliation? Do you think we have nothing better to do than go from one stranger's house to another? Basic courtesy. That's all.'

I imagined looking back and finding this mix-up hilarious, but Anita's mother had sounded narrow and squeezed as she talked about it.

Appa made a noise that was somewhere between a 'hmm' and an 'I see'. Now the other men were staring at their feet. Anita's father was also nodding but it was near-imperceptible.

'We were shocked,' Appa said.

'You were shocked for over three weeks? You had three weeks and you didn't think once that you should come talk to us?'

After some more silence, Amma was the one who spoke. 'We went to the police and tried to get the video removed. We are also trying some other ways.'

'Too many people already know,' Anita's mother said. 'That's how we found out. Everybody knows. Our relatives know. Our friends know. Those who don't know will find out soon enough. Who cares if it's removed now? People won't stop talking.'

Mohan said, 'We certainly understand your shock. This is one of the worst things that could have happened. In a hundred years, I would never have expected our family to be caught up in this sort of situation.'

Anita's mother adjusted her watch. Her husband maintained the same sullen expression as before.

'Of course, we are also trying a few things to get it removed,' Mohan said. 'A lawyer, maybe. There's been some talk of a private firm as well.'

'How old is your son?' Anita's mother asked.

'Twenty-two,' Amma said.

'If he's not here, where is he?'

'When this happened, we –' Amma hesitated '– we asked him to leave.'

'Is he still in town?'

'Yes.'

'Is Anita with him?'

'We don't know.'

Appa glanced at me. Anita's mother and all the others turned my way as well.

'I don't know,' I said.

I hadn't been to Sree's place in three or four days and the last time we'd texted was on Thursday evening. I felt confident that they were together now but I didn't say it.

'Can you call him and find out?' Anita's mother asked.

I looked at Appa and Amma and said, 'I called him half an hour ago. It was switched off.' This wasn't a lie.

'Try again anyway.'

'Yes, that's a good idea,' Mohan said.

I pulled out my phone and dialled Sree's number. Thankfully, it said the same thing as before. I turned on the speakerphone.

'Switched off,' I said.

'How long have they been together?' Anita's mother asked me.

'I'm not sure. Four years, maybe.'

'Four years. And are there other videos out there that we don't know about?'

I shook my head.

Mohan asked, 'They didn't know each other before university?'

'No. Classmates.'

I was relieved when Anita's mother turned to Appa and Amma. 'Did you know about their relationship?'

'No,' Amma said.

Appa pressed his hair back. 'Like I was saying, this whole thing has been a shock for us as well.'

We entered another patch of silence. It was broken by Mohan. 'You have a family business?'

'Yes,' Amma said. 'Textiles. We have a few outlets.'

'Veena here is a chartered accountant. Ravi has worked at the Life Insurance Corporation for – how many years now? Ravi?'

'What?' Anita's father said.

'How many years have you worked at LIC?'

'Twenty-six.'

'I see,' Amma said.

'Myself, I was in the railways. Now retired. And what does your son do?'

'He's studying to be a chartered accountant as well.'

93

'He has passed his IPCC?'

'Yes.'

'Good marks?'

'Yes. First attempt.'

'That's hard work. So now finals.' Mohan turned in my direction. 'And this is your younger son.'

'He's doing an internship. Journalism.'

Mohan seemed like he was about to ask another question, but Anita's mother cut him off. 'What do you think we should do here?' she asked.

'We tried to get the video removed,' Appa said. 'I think now with your help –'

Anita's mother held up a hand and said, 'No, that's not what I mean.'

She started to say something then stopped and veered to a different point. 'We'll need the address of the place where your son is staying. And also his number.'

'It's a house, yes?' Mohan asked me.

'Yes.'

'Rented?'

'A friend is letting him stay.'

'The friend is there with him?'

'I don't know, no.'

'We'll get somebody to visit now,' Mohan said. 'Just to check and find out if Anita's there. I suppose she might be.' He frowned.

Appa didn't put up a fight. He said okay and got up to find a pen. After he searched the drawers for a couple of minutes, slamming things and throwing books around, I went to the cupboard and found one for him. He passed it back to me. I considered refusing, then wrote down the address on the back of a receipt.

To Appa and Amma, Anita's mother said, 'You're okay with your son doing as he likes? I feel you'll also have some dignity. Some pride. I hope that's true?'

She took the piece of paper from me and gave it to Mohan without really looking at it. Without waiting for a reply either, she got up and started to leave. Anita's father and Mohan got up too.

Mohan seemed annoyed not to have been consulted about the departure. He said, 'Thank you, we just need to talk some things over in the car.'

Their car was a black Hyundai i20. A new model but plainly middle-class. If it had been a jeep or a van, my safety concerns for Sree would have doubled.

'Firstly, we just want to confirm Anita's whereabouts,' Mohan said.

As soon as they stepped out, Appa went to the bathroom, slapped his face with water, and stormed upstairs saying, 'Now let's get everyone else in this town to come over and lecture us.'

Amma sat down on the sofa. 'Your brother made his choices. We are the ones who have to live with it. Fate.'

Fifteen minutes later, I was dialling Sree and his friends while searching for my scooter keys – Appa had upset all the drawers. There was a knock on the door.

'She's with him,' Mohan said. 'We'll be in touch.'

Five minutes after that, my phone flashed Sree's name.

I answered by shouting at him. Something about not keeping us in the loop.

Sreenath didn't say anything.

Then he asked, 'What did they want?'

'Is Anita there?'

'They kicked her out.'

'I'll come over tonight.'

'Please don't.'

'Tomorrow, then.'

'Don't. Just call if you need something.'

'What did they say to you?'

'Some uncle of hers rang the doorbell and screamed for a while. Anita told him to leave us alone. What did they say over there?'

'I don't know. Lots of things. Mostly about not knowing where Anita was.'

'Okay,' he said. 'I have to go.'

I'd thought once Anita's parents found out, a certain foggy element would be lifted from our path. One burst and done – I thought we'd feel lighter. On the contrary, it seemed altogether too many people were involved now. That things would of course become messier and messier.

15

Sunday passed without incident. April–May was usually more dry, but appropriately now a typhoon was flying along the coast. Humidity pulled the air down. TV channels showed a lot of maps.

In the evening, I messaged Dhruti to ask if things were okay at Sree's.

Seems so, she said.

— *I wanted to go over, but he said he didn't want me to. Did you go?*

— *Best to give them some space, I think :)*

In another chat, a classmate from university, someone I barely talked to, was asking after everyone at home.

Much better now. All very cool, I said.

Major points to ur bro for gettin so lucky wid such a girl. Your goin to hav a tough tym catchin up. Im major jelous … He really did type like that.

I took a screenshot and sent it to Dhruti. A long time later, she replied with a one-worder saying, *People :/*

I thought of a few ways to pull the conversation forward but in the end gave up.

Monday night: some incident. Mohan came to the house alone. Sitting in the front room and drinking tea, he tried to talk about the video with Appa. 'Tried to' because both of them had a hard time circling into it. Mohan finally said that a nephew of his from NIT was advising on the matter. Then he moved on to zigzagging small talk about Royal Textiles, Sree, Anita, a recent health scare. What he said about Sree was: 'It's hard raising them. There are so many influences these days. What can you do? What can *we* do?' And about Anita: 'She had every chance to be a brilliant girl. Real potential, real brains. Who knows. People are more forgiving now.' Regarding the health scare, he said: 'So many tests, only for it to be benign.' Appa sat leaning forward, his arms crossed, politely answering questions or nodding along. Before leaving, Mohan said, 'In times like these, it's best if we put our heads together. That's all I'm saying.'

'I see,' Appa said.

Tuesday: Amma's younger sister rang to say that their cousin had received a call from a friend. Somebody had asked them about us on behalf of an anonymous party: caste, finances, background. I was out when this happened and Amma mentioned it to me only briefly, like it was nothing.

Wednesday afternoon: Mohan went by our shop and stayed for some twenty minutes, munching cashew biscuits in Appa's office. Appa was irritated. Mohan said he was in the area and wanted to ask Appa's opinion on a few lawyers. After that, he spoke at length about how tough their current predicament was, how bleak the future seemed, and how we *had* to act decisively. 'A lot of time has already gone,' he said.

On Thursday evening, we had a second visit from Anita's mother, with her husband and Mohan trailing behind. All three of them looked like they had been spending nights at Castle Dracula, especially Anita's mother. Her nose was running and she asked for some warm water. Anita's father was still wearing his lanyard from work. He kept tugging at it and, for some reason, mumbled, 'So that's where we are.'

This visit was short. The chit-chat part was powered entirely by Mohan. He really was a machine. If you fed him paper while he talked, you could shred the constitutions of at least three democracies in no time.

Anita's mother said, 'I don't want Anita living with some strange man just like that.' She wiped her nose on a kerchief and cleared her throat. 'You should talk to your son. Tell him they can't stay together like this.'

Appa spoke with more confidence now.

'Let me just tell you something first,' he said. 'We aren't on talking terms with our son. He doesn't live here any more. We don't give him money in secret. If you want your daughter to do something, isn't she the person you should talk to?'

Anita's mother turned to her husband. 'Imagine this.' She paused, and it looked like he was supposed to contribute. He scratched his ear instead.

Forcing a laugh, Mohan said, 'No no, everyone should speak their minds now. That's the best thing for all of us. Let's all speak frankly, even if it's a bit rude, it's okay. It's only the circumstances, nothing personal.'

Appa said, 'What I'm saying is the sad truth. I'm sorry if I offended, but it has nothing to do with rudeness.'

Anita's mother said she disagreed.

This started a back and forth, moderated by Amma and Mohan, that went on for a while and remained unresolved as Anita's mother got up and left.

The next morning I heard Appa and Amma discussing the possibility of talking to Sreenath, but as far as I know, nothing happened.

In between this, Appa found out about the fifty thousand rupees Amma had pledged to charity.

'School children?' he screamed, like they were his mortal enemies, always scamming him. 'Do you not have any sense? Why would you do this to me?'

'It's *our* money,' Amma shouted back. She mentioned the new TV. Appa said he'd bought it for *us*. I thought he'd throw something at it, but he must have remembered the bill.

Upstairs, I downloaded Tinder out of restlessness. There was a web designer near Infosys. A Punjabi tourist in Varkala. An NGO worker near Kollam. I expanded my search to Maximum Distance and slowly started reading each profile in bed. Then I downloaded Bumble and, later, Hinge.

16

Friday night saw bullet rain and thunder. The power kept tripping. Brown lakes formed everywhere. The tree in front of our house creaked and looked like it would fall at any moment.

Ominous, okay, but naturally I didn't think anybody would drive in this weather. And when nine thirty became ten, I thought we'd made it through another day. Then I heard the car pulling up outside. Appa, who'd been eating dinner, flung the rice sticking to his hands, washed up, and went to the door. Amma came down the stairs.

Anita's mother looked even more sleep-deprived, but her husband and Mohan seemed marginally better. She was wearing the same blue kurta as on her first visit. The brief run from the car to the house had drenched them. Despite leaving their shoes at the door, they tracked mud into the living room.

Anita's mother was angry, and not in the stern way she'd seemed earlier. This seemed like a confused, slippery anger. Her eyes were red and sunken. She kept exhaling loudly.

That, and the fact that they'd driven here late at night, through a literal storm, made me think we were finally going to get murdered.

'Another family friend called me today,' Anita's mother said, sitting down on the sofa. Her voice was frayed. At first I thought this was from the cold, then I thought she was going to cry.

'Someone who works in the building next to mine,' she said. 'Someone whose house we used to visit. Too many people know. How are we supposed to keep going?'

'We are in the same boat,' Appa said.

'What boat is that? We are drowning. It's different with a daughter. If you don't understand that, then I don't know what to say.'

'We can try going to the police again, maybe,' Amma said. 'Maybe we can all go and –'

Anita's mother snapped, 'Too many people know. How are you not understanding this?'

She looked at her husband and then at Mohan, as if to ask how they were tolerating this stupidity.

'I think –' Mohan began.

Anita's mother seemed to love cutting him off. In a clearer voice, she said something like, 'I don't want it to look like I have raised someone who goes around town doing whatever she wants with whomever she wants. And I can't sit around doing nothing to remedy this situation one way or another.'

'Okay,' Amma said. Appa was quiet.

This was when Anita's mother suggested that, at the very least, Sree and Anita should be married, now that things had gone this far. I don't recall her exact words but I do remember that it was blunt. She also said, 'We have been considering all options. This is how we feel and we don't want to waste any more time. Despite your initial lack of forthrightness, we believe you're good people with good intentions at heart.'

'Right,' Amma said. Appa was looking at Mohan and Anita's father.

'It's too late to save face, but this is the best we can do,' Anita's mother said. 'Not to mention that it's the responsible and honourable thing. What's expected of us as parents.'

'Right.'

For a lot of people who have grown up here in a certain middle-class background, this will likely seem procedural given the circumstances. Honour, Dishonour, Marriage, Redemption and so on. I'd had an idea that something like this might be asked of us. Appa and Amma must have thought about it as well, especially considering the angle of the previous visits and that call Amma's cousin got. In fact, looking back, they were almost certainly avoiding the subject, while on the opposite side, Anita's family tried to broach it.

Still, it did feel to me like we'd taken a sudden off-road from the main highway into a more ancient version of the city. It also seemed like we were veering away from solving the main problem that was the video.

Obviously I've never been in the sort of position Anita's mother found herself in. I imagine there's a lot of pressure. The need to maintain appearances and control. The temptation to make some quick-fix reparative gesture – the sort of thing you do when you feel helpless. Not to mention all the considerations they must have thought pragmatic. It would have seemed a no-brainer.

When I talked about this scene to some of my university friends, I cheesily added that I'd been watching Werner Herzog's *Cave of Forgotten Dreams* before Anita's parents had walked in. That it was paused on-screen, on the image of a prehistoric cave painting. That I wondered about how limited the perspective of the room really was in reference to everything out there, about how they were so lost in smallness. 'On the one hand, I kept thinking, these people are well-educated, they are university graduates. On the other hand, I knew it didn't matter, it was a lost cause.'

In reality, of course, the TV had been off and I'd seen the documentary a very long time ago.

Mohan cleared his throat. 'What has happened now completely destroys Anita's marriage prospects. I'm sure it's the same for your son. They like each other. They have been together for four years and are still together. They even live in the same house now. From our point of view, this seems very straightforward. They themselves will come to appreciate it in the future. Who else can they count on now but each other? What's more, when people ask us about the video, it'll at least be *something* if we can say they are husband and wife caught up in the wrong moment.'

'I see,' Amma said.

She must have been thinking about what we'd tell our relatives if this came to pass. Marriages were a big deal. We couldn't just slip it under the door and run away. We would have to give an explanation. At that point, I think a part of Amma must have still thought everything would disappear with time and some yet-unrealised effort, without more people knowing.

'Look,' Appa said. 'If it's our blessing you want, you have it, for all it's worth. But as I said before, it's not worth much. We aren't in touch with our son, we don't want to be in touch with him. And he most certainly won't listen to us. It's best that you talk to him directly and do whatever it is that you want.'

'That's not good enough,' Anita's mother said. 'Talking to him is not my job. That's yours. Frankly, I can't believe the way you're acting now. What your son has done is your responsibility. All this is your responsibility. Where we go from here is your responsibility. I should be making threats. I should be screaming. Instead, I come here trying to be civil and this is how you respond? Frankly, *you* should have been the one proposing this to *me*. Or is it something else? Now that your son has done this to our family, do you think we are bad? That you're too good for us?'

'We never thought anything close to that,' Amma said.

I wasn't so convinced.

Appa leaned forward and kneaded his eyes with the balls of his palms.

'This is about decency,' Anita's mother said. 'Talk to your son today. Tell him whatever you have to. But at this point, I don't have nearly as much patience as you might think I do.'

Anita's mother got up and walked to the door. It was still raining so much that later I'd find a frog on the windowsill outside my room.

'We'll be in touch,' Mohan told Appa. 'This is a tough time for all of us. We have all just been in a state of utter breakdown. Tempers have been high. But I'm confident that we'll come to an understanding. We'll all feel better about this soon.'

Anita's father, as usual, didn't say anything. He was staring at the floor and only moved when Mohan touched his shoulder. Going by the way he seemed right then, I thought there was a fifty to sixty per cent chance he'd hang himself by his lanyard.

After they left, Appa and Amma stayed up late talking in the living room. While Amma was unsure about what to do, Appa's idea was that we do nothing. He'd latched on to what Mohan had said in the end – 'we'll come to an understanding' – and taken it to mean that Anita's mother was simply blowing off steam, that she would go home, take rest, and wake up to reality.

17

My internship had come to an end earlier that week. On Saturday I went to the office, where I'd only been five times before, and collected my experience certificate. Many of my batchmates had bagged placements. I didn't even stick around to talk to the editor, and anyway, he seemed agnostic about my existence.

Instead, I drove to Zam Zam, ordered two greasy shawarmas, and scrolled my phone. While eating, I applied for a job in Vietnam as a production assistant on an Indian film set. It was something that showed up on a Media Jobs Facebook page. Hanoi was 6,569 kilometres from Trivandrum. And actually, you could even get there by road.

Headlines back at Blue Hills: Anita's mother had called. That morning, Mohan had gone over to Sree's place – apparently to check on Anita. He'd mentioned the proposal. Sree had said no and some other rude things before slamming the door so forcefully Mohan claimed hearing loss.

Amma was sat by the phone staring into a snow globe of the Taj Mahal.

When Appa heard, he complained about how the warehouse roof had started leaking and water had got into some of the goods. 'Those are real problems, our problems,' he said. 'Whatever they want to do with Sreenath, that's not something we should be concerned about. That's over.'

My instinct was that if it weren't for this wedding business, Appa might have cooled off on Sree by now and, in due time, even asked him to return home.

Sree didn't look unhappy to see me. Or maybe he was just relieved it wasn't someone else.

'Switch on your damn phone,' I said, stepping inside.

'I can't find the charger.'

'Bullshit.'

He was back to wearing his Cadet Corps shirt. The top two buttons had fallen off, which gave him a disco-villain look.

'I didn't get a placement,' I said.

'What placement?'

'Never mind.'

Anita was on the living-room mattress, shrouded in a blanket and propped up by three pillows and the wall. On her face was a wet towel. She squinted through one eye and said, 'Hey. What's up?' She looked like one of those Buddhist statues they uncovered in the mountains.

I asked her if she was okay.

'Yeah, just crawling out of a terrible migraine. I'm better now. Don't mind me.'

Sreenath seemed to have cleaned the house. All the bottles were gone and some parts of the floor were still drying. The curtains were closed but afternoon light strained through, coloured pink.

He sat down by Anita's feet and began doodling on what I assumed was her sketchbook. I dragged the lone plastic chair and sat opposite them.

'What did this Mohan person say to you?'

'Completely random things,' Sree said.

'They were over at our place talking about it. Find your charger. What did you tell him?'

'To mind his own business.'

'In those words?'

'No, but close enough.'

'You slammed the door in his face.'

'He kept trying to get inside.'

'They called Amma after that.'

Sree kept drawing.

From under the towel, Anita said, 'Honestly, he's a bit of a jackass.'

'Did they make you leave home?'

Anita recited the story.

She'd been in her room when she heard the commotion down-stairs. A couple of relatives, including Mohan, were arguing. Her father climbed up the stairs. He appeared at her door, stared at her, then went into the master bedroom. He pulled suitcases down and started packing. Anita's mother came up followed by two of her aunts and another uncle. They went into the master bedroom as well. Anita's father was saying he was tired of all the anxiety, all the worry that came from being there. Now, more scrutiny. He said: 'I want to go back to my hometown. I want to live free.' Then he abandoned the suitcases, went downstairs, jumped in his car. In the process of stopping him, another relative also got in. They pulled out and floored it down the road.

Anita still wasn't sure this was because of the video. Her father had always hated living the way they did. He was distant growing up, but if they were ever simpatico on one subject, it was this. The main problem was that their house was surrounded by relatives from Anita's maternal side. Aunts, uncles, cousins, grandparents. Not next door, exactly. But separated only by short walkable dis-tances. And boy did they walk. Combined with their other traits, Anita called them 'The Troupes'. There had been frequent argu-ments about all this since forever. So the scene involving her father wasn't exactly new.

Anita's mother came into her room then went out. Two minutes later, her aunt arrived to question her. Did she know, how long had she known, who was it. Also why. Anita couldn't remember what she'd said or if she'd said anything at all. The aunt asked her to pack. She said, 'You'll have to stay at my house.

Your mother doesn't want to see you now.' All Anita could hear was the blood in her skull.

The aunt grabbed a bag herself and started going through her things, tossing some on the floor, packing others. Anita said she was staying put. She tried to talk to her mother. The bedroom door remained closed despite repeated entreaties.

The aunt continued packing. Anita had an emergency bag ready anyway. She grabbed it from under the bed, stuffed her laptop, phone and a notebook inside. A couple of minutes later she left the house and hailed an auto.

'Exeunt,' Anita said. 'Finito.'

She had peeled the towel off her face and placed it around her neck. 'Now we wait. Or don't.'

I noticed Sree moving his leg so it touched Anita's socked foot.

'Are you okay, though?' I asked. 'Overall?'

'I don't know what else I expected.'

She sat up and Sreenath said, 'You're going to puke.'

'I'm fine. My back hurts.'

It made me want to look away, seeing Sreenath concerned like that.

'Your mother seemed very *unhinged* when she came over,' I said. 'No offence. And your father was basically tuned out the entire time he was there.'

Anita just nodded and wore this expression of 'ah, interesting' – like everything I was saying was news from Jupiter.

'What are you guys planning to do?'

'What can we do?'

'Maybe they'll drop napalm on us,' Sree said. He hummed 'Ride of the Valkyries'.

Anita said, 'Back in first year, I wear a skirt that ends just below my knee. Two days later, this aunt, the same one who packed my bag, she comes home from *a shopping trip* with new clothes she thinks will suit me *better*. My mother thanks her every chance she gets for the next four weeks. Another time, at a wedding reception, this random moron I was talking to gets drunk and dedicates a song to me on the PA system. You should have seen the silence, the looks I got from the whole family. Apparently, I'd *giggled* too hard at his jokes. Fuck you, I laughed like a normal person. Giggled, my ass. And this is just the tip of the iceberg. It's fucking traumatic being a woman in this country. Anyway, I'm sure they all think what's happening now is the result of all those things put together. Fuck it all.'

Sree said, 'Maybe they'll go full right-wing and beat up couples on Valentine's Day.'

Anita didn't laugh. 'Who knows.'

'People in horrible arranged marriages trying to arrange marriages.'

Anita tied her hair and went to wash her face.

I said to Sreenath, 'Guess you're not coming home for a while, then?'

'Guess not.'

'Do you even want to?'

'Not really.'

'What the hell are you drawing?'

'A giant dick.'

'Nice, a self-portrait. I sent you two thousand rupees. On Google Pay.'

Sree didn't look up. 'Why? Who did you rob?'

'Internship. Part of my stipend.'

'I don't need it,' Sree said. 'Thanks, though.'

'Have you figured out some alternative system of commerce? Are you mining bitcoin on your shitty Lenovo?'

'I still have cash in my account. Plus Anita. Plus friends. Plus I'm going to get a job. Plus Anita's doing freelance.'

'Return it, then. I need everything I can get, now that I don't have a placement.'

'You say that like it's my fault.'

Anita came back and sat down next to Sree. 'I'm drawing something for Instagram. Slice of life. About that reception thing.'

She closed her eyes and spread the towel on her face.

I decided to stay longer. Anita continued being talkative even if most of the talk was propelled by anger. She also continued swearing a lot and saying things like 'exeunt'. I knew Sree wanted me to leave – he dropped about ten hints a minute.

Despite both of them acting like they didn't care, I gave them a more detailed description of what had happened at home. A small part of me thought Amma might have reached out to Sree, just to ask if things were okay. No chance.

The sun sank fast. I don't recall discussing anything in particular. Maybe because everyone was tired, I don't recall us fighting either, save for Sreenath being snippy. Instead we watched back-to-back episodes of *Karikku* on Anita's laptop. All three of us nearly fell asleep at one point.

In the evening Dhruti dropped by. Officially, I had now grown a very red crush on her. I was rapidly growing a lot of crushes around then: university friends, family friends, Trisha who was now in Bombay, this one baker girl I'd right-swiped on Tinder. It was a major cultivation and every day I was toiling in the fields. With Dhruti, there was the anime talk. The Instagram posts I kept seeing. The mental image of her looking up from those yellow forms, grinning with her dentist-approved teeth and saying, 'You want to do it?'

A random scene that kept coming to me involved the two of us getting dressed to meet Sree and Anita for brunch.

Dhruti now brought outrage and drama of her own.

She bounced a wave off Sreenath and me before turning to Anita and saying, 'Unbelievable.'

It seemed all of them had already heard about what Anita's family wanted.

'Cashews, almonds, pistachios,' Dhruti said, lighting a cigarette. 'It's all kinds of nuts.'

Sreenath said, 'Talking about it gives it credence.'

'It's nothing more than bullying. Just keep holding your ground. Everyone is on your side. Just no.'

What constituted 'everyone'? I imagined a set, all holding pom-poms and banners, that included Dhruti, Arjun Samurai, Joel,

Meghna, Anita's other MA classmates, her juniors and seniors, members of that magazine she edited, some of her Instagram followers, Sree's co-conspirators in all those half-ventures, admirers from school and university who liked him for his brashness, and the more sophisticated friends he'd made over the years.

Anita thanked her.

Dhruti said, 'Unless you guys want to go ahead, in which case, that's absolutely fine as well.'

'Why don't we have a couple of kids too, while we are at it?'

'I'm just saying. You guys are nearly twenty-three. This is your life. Anything you want to do is okay. It's on you.'

'We are not getting married,' Sree said.

'Yeah, like maybe in fifty or a hundred years,' Anita said.

'Yup.'

'Talking about it really does give it credence.'

Dhruti said, 'I mean, what happened, it isn't a big deal at all these days. Really. It's practically nothing. You should know that for sure. I'm not saying you don't, but –'

Sree groaned. 'She's going to start talking again about all the cam-girls she finds inspiring.'

'Don't interrupt her lecture,' Anita said.

'You assholes should pay me for my esteemed counsel.'

I was silently smoking during this exchange, but, really, a big part of me wanted Dhruti to stop riling things up and go on vacation for a couple of weeks.

Around half past six, a friend of Sree's showed up with pot. Reghu or Raghav, a name like that. He had speakers in his bag, was partial to Pink Floyd, and seemed to have no clue about the video. He talked a lot about the benefits of hydroponic marijuana.

Sree opened the curtains. Dusk threw long shadows on the floor. A couple of kids were racing cycles down the street. I'd enjoyed pot the four or five times I'd smoked before, and when I took a few puffs now, a slow warmth spread across my body. I've never been in a bathtub, but I imagine the feeling is similar.

A while later, Dhruti and the other guy were in the kitchen trying to engineer a bottle bong. I was keeping an eye on them from afar. 'Hey You' was playing on loop.

Anita said to Sree, 'I remember one time I was listening to this song. Second year of uni. I was on this minibus with the family, cousins and everything. I think it was on the way to some resort in Tamil Nadu. Everyone else was sleeping. My page had hit 2k. We were texting non-stop about a cartoon idea you had. That cow one, I think. Must have been the week after I got my grades too. It nearly made me dizzy, trying so hard not to fall asleep.'

I leaned back against the wall and scratched my hair against it. It felt nice, the hair thing as well as listening to them.

Anita then started talking about some Hindi movie and Sreenath chipped in with bits of dialogue he remembered.

My phone rang. Anita's mother. I answered.

She said: 'If your brother doesn't want to marry Anita, you have to do it. There's absolutely no other option. And it has to happen now. Your parents have agreed. Your brother will too.'

That last part was random daydreaming, of course. Sometimes the gravity of my longing was so immense that anybody and everybody got pulled into it. Anita and I living together, cooking spaghetti, making money off our art, not talking to the rest of the world.

Dhruti staggered into the room coughing, changed 'Hey You' to some song I didn't know, then plopped down right next to me. This time, I could clearly tell that her hair was a chemical mix of peach and chlorine. Apart from that, her clothes reeked of pot. Sweat too. Her eyes were bursting with red capillaries.

Before I could process my surprise, she punched me on my arm and said, 'It's good to see you relaxed for once. You're always so keyed up. Like an office manager. This is cool. You could be a cool loner-stoner type. It's nice.'

'My default vibe is Office Manager?'

Dhruti laughed, throwing her head back, and touched my arm again. 'I'm serious. You should try it more often. Maybe do yoga. You play football, right?'

'Not as often as I used to, but I do.'

'You look athletic. I've always wanted to play.'

'You're pretty athletic yourself. Must be the swimming.'

'A couple of us used to break into the pool hall in my apartment building. We used to spend whole nights there in the summer, reading, listening to music. A pool at night is its own world. Fun fun.'

'I wish I had a pool.'

'I'd really love to play football.'

Then suddenly coughing, spittle flying, Dhruti ran to the kitchen to make sure she didn't throw up.

I can show you the ropes.

I'm playing this Saturday.

Football is all about –

I have coached so many people they call me the –

You can play on my team. Any day.

You can play on my team any day.

But when Dhruti returned, Anita sucked her into some other discussion and Reghu/Raghav wouldn't stop talking to me about *The Division Bell* no matter how many of my moles and fingernails I inspected.

Half an hour later, Dhruti's cousin came to pick her up. She said to the room, 'Be well,' tripped on a wire, and left in a car that was humming 80s Bollywood.

In total, I must have stayed there for five or six hours that day – the longest I'd spent with Sree and Anita. It was late when I turned for home. Weaving through night-time traffic at full speed, I felt limber and pleasant. Cars and bikes almost brushed against me. Cold air filled my shirt.

I should have kept going.

The living room was a hard block of white light, and my parents were having a major discussion. Not only did my high sour, I felt instantly guilty about relaxing at Sree's place and then angry at them for being able to host such an atmosphere while all this was going on.

I squinted at the large envelope lying on the teapoy.

Appa told me Anita's mother had sent it. It contained their family's biodata – what each parent did, what their daughter's qualifications were, their caste – along with an old photo of Anita looking demure in a yellow salwar kameez.

IV

Errant Sons,
Bellicose Families,
Supercomputers

18

Despite the weighty envelope, when Anita's mother called on Sunday night, Appa only repeated the same statement as before: we had nothing to do with Sreenath. And as before, this only made Anita's mother furious.

When Appa couldn't handle it, he passed the phone to Amma. She said, 'But it's not just our son, it seems your daughter doesn't want this either.'

Mohan was the one who replied. 'Such situations are complicated. If your son is so stubborn, Anita will of course be reluctant to say yes. It's only natural. And I myself saw how rude and vehement his refusal was. Which is why it's so important that you talk to him properly. Right away.'

Did they really believe Anita was saying no because Sree had? It's possible. They must have also felt that it ought to be Appa and Amma who led this campaign: talking to Sreenath, making him agree, and making sure he made Anita agree.

Between Monday and Tuesday, Anita's mother called three more times asking for updates. Each time she mentioned somebody new who had found out about the video, and each time it sounded like she was pulling out more and more of her hair. Anita's family seemed to be a very social one, at least compared to ours. They knew everybody in town and everybody knew them.

The way she talked about the marriage in relation to this made it seem like it would undo all damage.

Meanwhile Appa stared into the TV and came up with strange solutions. 'What if we get an astrologer to say that the alliance is fatal for everybody involved?'

I don't know how serious he was, but Anita's mother didn't strike me as someone who'd let a wayward astrologer push her around. She'd simply have brought four or five of her own people and issued counter-statements. The envelope she'd sent hadn't even included a birth-chart.

During those two days, her demands transformed from being a scaffolded idea to something concrete and ready for occupancy. Eventually Appa and Amma decided they had to set aside their own aversion to the marriage and talk to Sreenath. It was Wednesday evening.

I called him from my number and tried to put them on. He said, 'If this is about that Mohan crap, forget about it. Come to think of it, I don't want to talk at all.'

Appa and Amma decided to visit him the following day.

This was a trip that I desperately wanted to avoid. In fact, I tried to shoot out of the house saying I had a job interview. Out of nagging concern or because of Amma's pleas – somehow – I was detained. When it was time to go, there I was, in the backseat of the car, travelling through the wet afternoon.

The atmosphere reminded me of our clammy car rides to PTA meetings. Back then, teachers would inevitably find some way to praise Sree whereas I was a 'moody pencil-smoker – distracted, never to be positioned near a window, and unwilling to live up to potential'. But still, Sreenath getting praised was relief enough for me. Not because I was such a great guy or anything, but because it cut the tension at home.

When we parked opposite his place now, Amma refused to budge.

'Both of you go,' she muttered, trying not to breathe too much. 'I'll watch the car.' We sat still for a while and scanned the scene. Even though Appa had been there before, he seemed surprised by the grazing dogs and the bright garbage on the roadside. We got out. Appa had asked me not to tell Sree we were going over. I'd texted him nonetheless but received nothing in reply.

It looked like he wasn't going to answer the door either. Then after about five minutes of continuous bell ringing, a slash appeared. Sree squeezed himself out and stood in the doorway, gripping the handle behind him. Appa took two steps back.

'What do you want?' Sree asked Appa's sandals.

'Why can't you just do it?' Appa was talking to the doorstep.

'That question itself is ridiculous.'

'Why does everything have to be so hard?'

'It's very simple, if you actually care. I don't want to do it because I don't want to.'

'If you weren't ready for the consequences, you shouldn't have done *any* of this.'

'These are not consequences. All this is just people being stupid. You're wasting your time talking to me.'

I saw Anita standing by the living-room window. Then Appa saw her too. Short-circuit.

'Do you know that the warehouse is flooding? There's water up to my ankles.' With that he lurched towards Sree as if to grab him. Sree jumped back and shut the door. Appa, now seemingly intent on defeating every door in the world, clobbered this one as well while I tried to hold him back.

One of two kids walking by said, 'Life didn't turn out the way you hoped, huh?'

Rubbing his bruised knuckle, Appa carried the rage home and decided to be proactive. He dialled Mohan and told him we had talked to Sree and done our best, that it wasn't going to work out, and that they were on their own now, good luck. Appa didn't even wait for his reply before putting the phone down.

19

We didn't get calls from Anita's mother on Thursday or Friday. I spent them sick after what had started off as static in my throat turned into a low-grade fever. On Instagram, I saw Dhruti had a fever too. The picture showed her lying in bed next to a row of pill-strips. In bleary thoughts, I remembered her coughing in my face and imagined I might now be possessed by her same germs. That I was feeling the shivers she was feeling and we were sharing something intimate. This fantasy was helpful and distracting because otherwise, aside from being sick, I was anxious about the zero calls. The air tasted metallic. The phone felt dangerous. Somebody should have cordoned it off and sent for the bomb squad.

What I would have loved was to enter cryosleep. As a child, I'd even decorated my bed one summer to look like a cryomachine. Dial set to 13000 HE. Flying cars and robot friends. A fresh start.

Back in the present, Anita's mother began dropping by. I don't think I'd be misrepresenting what happened next if I were to call it a haunting.

When she rang the bell on Saturday, I came down wrapped in a blanket, reading an article about online dating tips, and saw Amma peeking out from behind the curtains. 'I'll talk to her later, over a call,' she said to me. 'That's better.'

Anita's mother was only partly visible. She stood facing the door for five minutes, then glanced at the window where Amma and I were. She pressed the doorbell again. Amma asked me if the curtains were translucent. Five minutes became ten and the doorbell rang several times in between.

Anita's mother was wearing an emerald-green saree. She held her back and neck so straight, it looked like she was peering over an imaginary fence. Every few minutes she toggled between crossing her arms and standing still, and turning around to study the rest of the colony. Nothing in her demeanour suggested she would leave any time soon.

Finally, on minute fifteen, Amma pretended to be in a huff, like she'd just run downstairs, and opened the door. A very poor performance.

Anita's mother said: 'It's truly unconscionable that you would treat us like this after everything your son has done.'

'I was in the shower,' Amma said, perfectly dry.

'You thought I would go away.'

'Please don't call us liars. Maybe it's best for everyone if you phoned first.'

'So you can make excuses in advance?'

This was happening in full view of our neighbours. When Amma invited Anita's mother inside, she said she'd rather stay where she was.

Amma then tried getting emotional by repeating, in hammy detail, everything that had happened at Sree's place. The way we had begged him. The way Appa had lurched at him. The way Sree had shut the door.

'So?' Anita's mother said. 'If one visit doesn't do it, I suggest that you go over for as long as it takes till what you want is done.'

'Perhaps we should at least wait a few months. They might easily say yes then.'

'The longer I wait, the easier it becomes for you to talk your way out. Don't think I don't know this.'

'Do you really want to force together two people who don't even want to be together?'

'I don't want to do any of this. But I have to. Somebody has to. And what force? They are already together. They have been together for four years. They have already done things people do after they get married and they have done them in public. At this point, it's just a formality. This is what is best for everyone. It's the least they can do compared to the pain we suffer.'

To end the conversation, Amma said she would try harder.

Immediately, Anita's mother began following her own advice – she decided to come over for as long as it took, till what she wanted was done. Each day that following week, she rang the bell and asked if we had had a chance to work things out. She never stepped in, only argued on the doorstep, and left saying she'd be back.

Whenever the bell rang, I put my headphones on and tried not to listen. Even so, I did hear enough to know that her arguments weren't anything new. We weren't saying anything new ourselves. Appa had scolded Amma for promising to try again. Being firm was the only way, he said. The stance remained: 'I've already told Mohan everything there is to say. I suggest you talk to your daughter and whoever it is that you want her to marry and arrange things between them. It is simply out of our control now. Sorry.'

You would think that demonstrating such rude resistance would kill the idea of an alliance with our family. Not with Anita's mother. She became more determined. To her these were temporary hurdles. Salvation was within touching distance.

Amma called a marriage broker and tried to find interesting subsoil. She had done similar research before for some of her friends. Now Amma said she wanted to know exactly who we were dealing with. I think she also hoped to find some leverage to help with the resistance.

The broker phoned back with quick results.

Anita's father was about eight or ten years older than her mother – this wasn't rare with arranged marriages. It certainly wasn't a defect. On Anita's mother's side, they were mostly executives. Less glamorously, on Anita's father side, they tapped rubber and owned land just outside town. Altogether they were a big family. They were religious like Appa and Amma. Not rabid. Also like

Appa and Amma. We already knew they were the same general caste as us, where they lived, what they did. So far, nothing interesting from Amma's point of view.

The broker said, 'But wait.'

Only a few years earlier, Anita's father had had a gambling problem. This was around the same time that Anita's mother was planning to start her own accountancy firm. Anita's father had been so talented at amassing debt that Anita's mother not only had to kill her plans and empty their savings, but also borrow from relatives. The debt was of course fully paid now, though it had given them a bad name and generated gossip. Some relatives had wondered if it was even possible to owe so much from gambling alone. One of the juicier, more unsubstantiated theories involved the idea of Anita's father having a second family.

'And that's not all, not even close,' the broker said. 'Their daughter. This you won't believe. Huge, huge, huge problem there. Avoid. At. All. Costs.'

Then, not having bothered to check who the other person in the video was, he brought us full circle and happily billed us five thousand rupees.

'And for what?' Appa asked Amma. 'What in the world did this achieve?'

I think the gambling story made Appa feel more sympathetic towards Anita's mother. Poor entrepreneurial, ambitious woman struck down by someone else's incompetence – and that too, twice. Appa disliked feminists but liked women who shared Indira Gandhi's straight spine and dictatorial bent.

For me, what the broker said threw some light on the parts of Anita's home life she'd never mentioned and that Sree had only hinted at.

On the whole, it may have made things worse.

Amma didn't know how to put the gambling information to practical use. But one day, about five visits in, she thought: It's not like their problems began with us. Amma felt suddenly empowered to ignore the door even as the bell kept ringing.

Next time, instead of coming to the door and talking to us,

Anita's mother parked her car opposite our house and simply sat inside, pecking at slabs of papers with a blue pencil.

When Amma approached her, she said she was doing her work and waiting for us to do what we ought to do. Then she rolled up the window and got right back to it.

This began happening again and again over the days that followed. Sometimes Anita's mother would stay for as long as three or four hours. Often the radio would be playing. Always, her clothes, her hair, her make-up were immaculate. The time she was in that car felt like a physical expanse, as though we had to hike from one minute to the next.

'Let her sit there as long as she wants,' Appa said. 'Keep ignoring it.'

While earlier I'd called the marriage proposal 'procedural', I certainly didn't think pushing so hard fell inside that bracket. In fact, now I couldn't quite believe this was happening to us, that such things happened so easily. Why wasn't someone stopping her? What was she going to do next? Then I wondered, watching her stone face and the way she sat in that small front seat, if she might have been thinking of herself as a protestor or a martyr, sacrificing her life for a cause that those concerned couldn't appreciate just yet. Maybe she thought people would admire her grief. Or at least that they'd stop blaming her and the way she had raised her daughter – as even Amma seemed to – and see her as a victim rather than as a perpetrator. Maybe, having suffered one instance of humiliation brought on by her husband, she didn't want to submit so easily to the next one brought on by her daughter. In that sense, it seemed possible to me that her display was a pure outpouring of rage, disconnected from any plans towards a useful end. Maybe she didn't even expect an actual 'yes'.

'Sometimes you notice lunatics in traffic,' Appa said. 'They must all belong to some home or the other. Occasionally, you meet them in person.'

The residents of our colony were sensitive to outsiders. Security called Amma asking if they should keep letting Anita's mother in. Some people had made enquiries about the Hyundai i20 emitting

Red FM. We could have said no, but Appa and Amma were too worried that she would make the scene worse. What if she stood in front of the main gate screaming, or created problems at the shop? The master plan was to tire her out without escalation. I also suspect that my parents had started seeing themselves as delinquent and irresponsible. They must have thought too that everyone who heard about the case would only take the side of Anita's mother and call them a cheat.

During this time, Amma didn't leave the house once. And when the car was parked outside, she didn't even leave the top floor – like existing on a different plane to Anita's mother made her feel more protected.

Appa too stayed home when he could, though he walked all over the place.

To Mohan, he said on the phone, 'Is this the way to go about it?'

Mohan gave a very tepid response, saying things weren't good at their house and that it was natural for a mother to react so passionately. Had we not seen the contents of that video?

'What's next,' Appa said. 'Soon you'll be sending goons to beat us up.'

Amma was in two minds. Sporadically, she had started dialling Sree's phone and begun asking me for news from his side. Sree would cut her calls and submerge for several hours. On the day that he finally picked up, Amma asked, practically, 'How are we supposed to live like this?'

20

I was by then carrying buckets and buckets of news from home to Sreenath's place. In the beginning, my frustration and disbelief were aimed entirely at Anita's mother, but it was only a matter of time before she started to seem like an entity that was beyond the reach of reasoning and communication. Like bad weather. Soon I was more angry at what I perceived to be Sree and Anita's refusal to help us tackle the situation.

Outwardly I tried to remain calm. And I never went over with a particular agenda in mind, though every now and then I did ask if they couldn't just get married and save us. Sometimes they'd shrug this off or act like they hadn't heard me. Other times it would lead to quarrelling, especially if I grew persistent.

Sree liked to mime the inhalation motion with his hands. 'Can you take a deep breath first?' It was easy to dislike him.

Anita told me her parents wouldn't talk to her. Her contact with home was through Mohan and gang. She had tried saying all manner of things, and angrily counted them out on her fingers: Thumb) That Sreenath had already agreed to the wedding but she was never going to, so Anita's mother should stop visiting our house and talk to Anita alone; Index) That Sree and Anita would get married later, in two years' time, maybe even a year's time; Middle) That Sree and Anita had actually broken up; Ring) That Sree had been seeing someone else for a while; Pinky) That if they were to get married now, they'd simply go and get divorced two months later; Other Thumb) That they would contact the police if this went on; Other Index) That they were depressed and would do something drastic.

Whatever it was, the opposing camp either refused to believe her or didn't care. What they came back with was 'Please give it more thought', 'We have your best interests at heart', 'You simply cannot see the future the way we can', 'Sure, if after two months you want to get divorced, go right ahead, but listen to us for now' and 'Please don't do anything to make the situation worse for everybody because of some misguided principle. Just think about it.'

I don't know if Mohan was trying to go along with Anita's mother or if he really stood by all of this. Anita didn't know either. At the end of the day, she seemed as clueless about everything as I was.

When she still told me her mother would back off any time now, I said, 'Kindly remove your head from your ass.' Sreenath tried to escort me outside. Years under Appa's tutelage had perfected my shouting voice. 'Why can't you just look at the bigger picture for once?'

'I have seen it,' Sree shouted back. 'It's fucked up and it's fucking humiliating. Who gets married like this? What the fuck is this?'

I agreed, but 'What about all the humiliation Appa and Amma have to go through? Are you even capable of thinking about other people? Every day is a pain.'

I turned to Anita. 'How about if you just pack up and go home? That might calm them down. Just go home and stay there.'

'I'm not doing that. It won't change anything anyway. The best thing to do is just sit tight and wait for everything to subside. It will.'

Sree said, 'Maybe we'll just run away and get lost altogether.'

'Yeah? And leave us to deal with that mess too?'

I don't recall everything I said in those days, but most visits started with me supplying updates. Sometimes I tried to discuss unrelated things. More often than not, it devolved. I was always surprised by the fact that they allowed me in, even if they didn't let me stay long.

Sree and Anita smoked voraciously and the air was all haze. The floor was filthy. Apparently certain species of cockroaches love to eat cigarette ash. Poor Meghna. Her uncle in Qatar had heard about the house being used for exile, and why. He wanted it cleared out as soon as possible.

What are the indicators of two people going through a very stressful time? The mess, of course. A headache that seemed to rally between Sree and Anita. A disregard for hygiene. Weight-loss in Anita's case. Weight-gain in Sree's. Dead eyes for both. No sleep.

They seemed to be retreating more and more into the bunker. I think after those first few calls home, Anita had stopped talking even to Mohan.

Their friends seemed to be keeping back too. Maybe they'd been told to do so. I was glad no one was around. Despite the fact that I would have liked to run into Dhruti, I didn't want her seeing me the way I was. In my head, Dhruti would have wanted me staunchly on Sreenath's side, the obviously right side.

On one occasion, the exchange between Sree and I was so blitzing, the shouting so rapturous, I felt I was having an out-of-body experience. Standing opposite me, Sree looked equally stunned. His face was swollen blue. Anita was watching us from the table, massaging her palms the way she'd learned on YouTube. It was supposed to alleviate stress. I high-kicked a full bottle of Minute Maid and walked out swearing as juice spilled everywhere.

When Sreenath still let me in the next morning, that's how I realised they were likely going to settle.

Back home, Anita's mother was parked outside looking at her papers. Appa was sitting at the dining table surrounded by tax forms, drawing what looked like a daisy on his arm. Amma had gone one level higher than usual. She was on the roof airing blankets. Her eyes were watery from the sun. She skipped lunch and went to bed.

Later that night, I saw news reports of a family who'd been

smothered by a landslide. I felt ashamed that we were all fighting over such nothing, that our problems were so artificial.

Appa said, 'Well, at least they are at peace. God is great.'

That was also the night Sree answered Amma's phone call. It was the first time he'd talked to her since leaving home. Even though he still maintained that Anita's mother would cool off, Sreenath sounded more worried.

The next day, I thought I could make a real difference. Like Kendall Jenner in that ad where she stops riots by serving Pepsi, I took a cup of tea and went over to Anita's mother as she sat in her car. I said, 'Aunty, such things don't matter as much as you think they do. People simply don't care. Do you know what all is going on in the world at this very minute? Today in Agra, a thirty-year-old man –' She rolled up the windows and looked straight ahead.

21

It must have happened on Anita's mother's tenth or eleventh sit-in, though to me it felt more like the fortieth or fiftieth one. Appa, reversing our Civic out of the porch, miscalculated the arc of his turn and bumped into her car. Anita's mother got out and began yelling. 'Have I become so invisible that you're now driving *through* me?' Then she went on to accuse us of having no humanity or honour, of purposefully trying to humiliate and intimidate her.

'It's only a bump,' Appa said, touching the side of her car. 'Look.'

There had been a thunderstorm the morning before. Anita's mother pointed to the creaky tree in front of our house and said, 'Yesterday that could have fallen on me and crushed me. I could have died. Is that what you wanted? You just let me sit here!'

Amma and I had come out of the house at the same time as our neighbours. Karthika aunty's husband asked us if everything was okay. Amma tried to keep everyone back, smiling like all this was part of some clever misunderstanding. Most of the colony must have known about Sree and the video. But now I felt we were quickly becoming a public nuisance.

'Let's discuss this inside,' Amma told Anita's mother.

'I'm waiting right here, and when I leave, I'm coming right back.'

Anita's mother got in the car and, as promised, stayed for

another hour before finally driving away. Our house was silent. The whole colony seemed silent. Wherever Appa had planned to go, he postponed it. Amma paced the runway between the front door and the kitchen. A few times she picked up the phone and put it back down. I went upstairs and tried to read the paper.

It was at noon that Amma made me take her to Sree's house. We went in an auto. The sky was low and dense. I could smell the sea, and then, closer to Sreenath's place, fresh sewage.

This time he opened the door right away. Anita was standing a few steps behind him. Amma glared at both of them, but mostly at Anita. Of all the times to be wearing one of Sree's shirts. I think Amma blamed her for a lot, including Sree's current stubbornness. Not based on any actual reasoning, just maternal bias.

Amma said, 'I'm tired. This can't go on. You'll just have to do it.'

Sree seemed taken aback by Amma's presence in the house. Anita wouldn't meet her eye.

'It's just so stupid and senseless, Amma,' Sree said. His voice had become whiny. 'It's unreal. What will we even tell people?'

'Tell them what you want, it's the only proper thing to do.'

Sree grabbed two fistfuls of his hair and groaned.

First the anxious discovery of the video, then getting thrown out, then all this pressure, the viral nature of the thing itself, an uncertain future –

Over the past couple of weeks, I had started to think of Sreenath as a fully-grown adult, not twenty-two but thirty or thirty-five. But in that moment he looked like a school boy.

Amma said, 'Do you want me to kill myself? Because that seems like the only other option.'

'Yeah, sounds great,' Sree said. 'Go for it.'

Anita took off her glasses and wiped them on her shirt.

Amma wouldn't say anything more, so Sree groaned again and turned my way. I wish I had kept quiet.

'Everybody's had enough,' I said. 'Just say yes already.'

'It's not like we have an actual choice,' Anita said.

22

Appa and Amma made phone calls to five or six of our close relatives. All of them would find out soon enough; it was better if they heard the news from us.

Amma spoke to the women and Appa spoke to the men. It seemed that being with the video for so long had helped them grow the sort of vocabulary that this task needed.

'There's been a minor problem': that's how Appa began each call. Followed by:

'Apparently somebody has found a photo or a clip or something, some nonsense, we don't know, it's all quite strange, but –'

'Compromising circumstances', 'mistakes', 'unfortunate', 'carelessness'. Appa made them work for details. If they persisted, the phrase 'only ourselves to blame' was brought out.

After five minutes of this, Appa would say, 'So, we talked to the girl's family and we all felt that the best way to move forward was to help them get married. Now they'll be there for each other, and of course, it's the right thing to do as well.'

Appa would then go on to praise Anita's family, calling them virtuous, understanding and reliable. He'd also inject that the ceremony was going to be small and that, given the circumstances, we weren't inviting anybody.

Appa's mother wasn't told much. She was eighty-seven, close

to senility and bliss. Amma's parents had no grasp of anything technological. Appa told them a great many things at once, including that someone had morphed certain pictures using advanced supercomputers. He didn't specify what kind of pictures these were and left them with the bottom line: 'But it's all been solved now.'

Our relatives were understandably shocked. Reluctant to question Appa and Amma, they called me. Maybe they meant well but each person had their own opinion of where we had gone wrong. Everyone was an internet expert. Everyone knew how to deal with errant sons and bellicose families. Of course, everything they had to say, we had already considered ourselves. I tried my best not to be rude. It seemed that our family had sunk to a lower status. I overheard Appa saying that being so low meant people were inclined to give us advice and we had no choice but to listen and say thank you like they'd just changed our lives.

After one end of the family knew, it wasn't long before everyone did. From distant cousins to Appa's old co-workers. They would call and say, 'Listen, there's a rumour going around and we just wanted to bring it to your attention.'

Still, with the ceasefire declared and the confession done, I think Appa and Amma slept better.

After that day with Amma, Sree didn't really talk to me. If he talked to Amma or Appa, it was only when such conversations were unavoidable or involved some logistical detail. Not that they were itching to talk to him either. Their embarrassment had been refreshed from more people finding out.

Mohan played liaison. Before the week was over, a date had been picked.

During those days, I was always out wasting petrol going nowhere. I received a few mails about job interviews, but didn't follow them up and kept my phone turned off. I got a haircut and, when that didn't feel right, another haircut. I wanted a new look. For the first time I also said yes to a deep-clean facial and a pedicure. Everything continued to be grubby.

Occasionally, friends called. If they happened to mention the video, I took the opportunity to ask them how they thought their families might react in a similar situation. This wasn't a challenge in any way, as some thought. I just genuinely wanted to know.

23

The wedding happened in a small yellow room at the registrar's office in Pattom. Aside from Anita's parents, two of their relatives were also present. Our side had Appa, Amma and me – even this seemed too much. Earlier that morning, Appa had tried to avoid the function by complaining about his frozen shoulder. Now he seemed to be having telepathic conversations with all the dust-covered objects in the room. He'd stare at the lamp for a while, then the printer, then the winter-world paperweight, then the lamp again. Standing next to him, Amma kept blushing.

It was a hot day. There was no mingling to speak of. A woman asked Amma what Appa did for a living, though surely she must have known. Amma told her anyway and that was it. Everyone was dressed in casuals. The only exception was Anita's mother who'd worn a bright saree. That too was nothing special. Now that the wedding was actually happening, it seemed like she didn't know what to do with herself. In front of the people she'd brought, she acted happy and relieved. She must have felt compelled to do this – after all, she'd pushed so hard and put everybody through so much. It had better count for something.

Anita's father was sombre and distracted. From what I gathered, it wasn't that he was opposed to any of this. Just annoyed that they'd dragged him in. When some shuffling brought us next to each other, I saw a sweat map of Russia spreading across his back.

'You took a leave from school?' he asked me.

'I just finished university, uncle.'

'I see.'

'It happened a while back, actually.'

'I see. Which school is that?'

'Oh. I was talking about university. Not school.'

He opened a button of his shirt. 'Do you know why, in government offices, these fans are always set to such a low speed?'

'No, uncle.'

He stared at them. 'It must be so papers don't fly about. They deal with lots of loose sheets.'

'Yes, good observation.'

Mohan delivered Sree and Anita in a taxi five minutes after the rest of us had got there. Sree was wearing a blue T-shirt and black trousers. Anita was wearing her black hoodie and jeans. Half of me had hoped they wouldn't actually come. Now that they were here, I felt like I had one too many organs inside me.

'Do you need anything?' I asked Sreenath.

'No.'

Up close, both of them smelled of wine. They also looked unsteady. I could picture them standing in the hallway of their house, inverting a bottle just before getting into the car. The rest of the room didn't seem to sense this. Either that or they acted like they couldn't.

Anita ignored everyone. Her mother tried to say something to her about her hair being loose. More than a white flag, this felt like a feigned interaction for the sake of those gathered. Anita turned the other way and coughed into her hand. Her father, who was standing there, didn't even look at her.

Once during a heated discussion at Sree's place, Anita had sprung to her mother's sudden defence. 'Yes she can be frightening, but she's not *literally* stupid or deranged. When I was a kid, I used to admire the way she handled things. She's not *evil*. In a few days, she will calm down and see sense.'

For good measure, Anita had dispensed a story from when she was fourteen. It concluded: 'And even though I had shown no prior interest in music or drumming and even though it was clear I was only doing it so I could be near Fatima's so-called girlband, my mother still took me around the city, on a busy day, in the middle of a busy year, to look at second-hand drum kits like it was the most urgent thing in the world.'

Perhaps Anita had said all this only to emphasise the need for inertness and patience. Anyway, now she looked betrayed.

For the most part, people stayed quiet. Only Mohan kept saying stupid things like: 'Whatever has happened thus far, let's believe it's all been for the best. What we want to do now is hope for good things, here on out.'

'Here on out' was hard to imagine. Amma had told me that Anita's family meant for them to move to Chennai in the near future, once Anita finished her MA – classes had ended even before the video and now she only had to submit her dissertation. In Chennai, she could start working at a family friend's accounting firm. If Sree wanted, he could continue his studies, transfer to another articleship, and join another CA institute in the city. Otherwise, they would help him find a job as well.

The change of location was meant to give them some breathing room. In the meanwhile, Mohan had rented them an apartment that wasn't too far from where Anita's parents lived.

After I talked to Sreenath, Amma asked me, 'What did he say?'

'Why will he want to say anything?'

Sree and Anita had dark faces. They stood deliberately apart and I didn't see them look at each other once the entire time. When Anita's hand grazed Sree's, both of them flinched.

Thankfully, the ceremony itself wasn't much more than a bureaucratic signing of documents and some stamping. Mohan took a few photographs on his phone.

When we stepped out, the rest of the morning was still there. It was cloudy. I had the feeling of leaving a movie theatre – like I had witnessed something that happened outside of real life and didn't count for much.

Appa, Amma and I watched Sree and Anita as they got into the waiting taxi and went back to their old place. Mohan rode in the front seat.

Anita's mother looked like she wanted to come over and say something, but in the end she got in her own car and fled the scene.

24

Appa's reaction to the wedding day was to sulk at Sree's desk; Amma took herself to a nearby temple, marching out of the house like she was going to demand a refund.

I went to the football ground at my old school and played a particularly brutal match for four hours. I got elbowed in the chin, skinned a lengthy knee, and nearly popped an eyeball.

The other phase of my reaction involved calling Dhruti and asking her if she wanted to have coffee with me. I'd decided to do this as soon as I left the registrar's office. Throughout the football match, I'd replayed our encounter at Sree's place so much, examined it so finely – the laughing, the arm-touching, the spark in her eye, the banter; and maybe this explained the injuries – that by the time I got home, I was certain she would agree to meet right away, even if Sree had happened to rant to her about my being some kind of a traitor and a nuisance. It seemed to me that if I could take her through everything that had happened at our house since the day of the new car, and if she listened and understood, I would feel immensely light and immediately capable of digesting the whole episode. I even imagined her nodding with concern and saying, 'Such things are difficult. Poor you. Wow. Also, what happened to your face?'

In my room, I set down a glass of water, cleared a space on my bed, and made sure my phone had at least seventy per cent charge. That's how long I thought the call would be. I dialled her. Dhruti answered and I realised first thing that she hadn't even saved my number. Then, when I clarified who it was, she said, 'Oh – hello,' in a dull way that made me take a seat and drink the prepared water.

In contrast to her greeting, the background of her house was full of noise and colour. I heard the sound of dinner plates, music and, over all that, a thick layer of voices.

I charged ahead and asked her about the coffee. Dhruti said, 'Sadly, I haven't got any more updates from the police guy. I called him yesterday. Apparently, there was some high-level hack at VSSC. Somebody stole some rocket stuff and it's just complicated all their lives.'

Compared to the last time I'd heard her speak – when she was high – her voice was now flat with lots of sharp corners.

I said, 'Do you want to meet and have a coffee anyway?'

A woman called out to Dhruti. She muffled her phone and answered brightly for several seconds before coming back on. 'Sorry?'

'I was just asking if you wanted to get coffee anyway. To catch up.'

The background seemed to grow even louder. What were all these people doing that was so fun?

Dhruti said, 'Ah, I'm not sure I have the time this week, no.' The 'Ah' she made was several feet long.

I also noticed that she didn't propose an alternative date. That didn't stop me.

'How about next week, then?' I said. 'I just came back from the wedding and I don't know if Sree told you anything, but I was there for a while helping out. It's awful. Though I suppose what happened in the end was just a pragmatic truce –'

I was gaining momentum when I realised Dhruti had moved away from her phone. The same woman from earlier was asking her if she knew where the white cups were. The music had changed to Michael Jackson's 'Thriller'.

Michael Jackson on a day like this. I suddenly felt Dhruti was a pretender who'd stuck around Sree's place and kicked up a fuss only because it brought her to the centre of the action. Now she was dancing to pop while the rest of us, the ones who really cared and had really tried to help, were eating fire. She didn't even have the courtesy to go into a quieter room. Surely there must have been a room that was quieter than the one she was in. Surely the white cups could wait two minutes. At the very least, she could have suggested that I call back later. I wondered if she was showing off her jubilance. I also wondered why, after likely knowing about the wedding already, Dhruti wasn't being more sympathetic. Was I being excluded from said sympathy?

When she returned, Dhruti's voice carried a smile, like she was still amused by whatever joke she'd heard over there. 'Sorry again, what were you saying?'

I downed the rest of my water and remembered that she'd called me an office manager. At the time it had seemed charming, now not so much. 'I was *asking*. How about next week? For the coffee?' Then I added, to imply she was in dereliction of duty: 'The police guy you mentioned, I was hoping we'd have *something* by now. Because I was over at Sreenath's place recently, just helping out, and –'

A plate broke or maybe I shattered a white cup with the power of my mind. I thought I heard Dhruti laugh. Someone started singing 'For He's a Jolly Good Fellow' in the loudest voice possible.

I said, 'Fuck it, never mind, hope you have fun,' and hung up.

My battery was still at seventy per cent.

Honestly, I thought there was a good chance she'd call me right back and ask if everything was okay. For the two hours that followed, I did nothing but angrily check WhatsApp. Each time I saw zero notifications, I achieved a new level of depression. Finally I called her. She didn't answer. Then I left a generic, if somewhat passive-aggressive, apology about not being in a good headspace. No reply. I deleted the apology. Maybe I'd confirmed for her the things Sreenath might have mentioned. Or maybe she'd thought, What the hell is his problem? and then gone about her evening.

The smell of Amma's incense was filling the house. Amma

usually lit incense only on very important but sad days. On the morning before a difficult maths exam. Or two hours before results. The Pavlovian response it triggered was a mixture of dread and helplessness.

I crawled into bed and pressed my sore face against the headboard. My room shared a wall with Sreenath's. Often he'd hammer at it to register a noise complaint. When incense was lit, he'd shout, 'Put that out right this instant. You have turned the air radioactive.' Everything was quiet now. More than ever, it hit me that Sreenath was out of the house, and officially, legally, part of something else.

Two days after that, I heard from Joel that Dhruti and Arjun Samurai were together. Apparently, it had happened a while back. They had entered our terrible orbit, hung out at that house, cracked jokes, got closer to each other, and somehow used our scandal to fuel their romance. Now they were going around town in Arjun's blue Santro. It shouldn't have affected me much, really. I'd hardly known Dhruti. I'd barely talked to her. My crush on her was imaginary. Asking her to coffee had been a function of impulse.

Still, for the rest of the week I refused to get out of bed. At some point Amma came into the room, diagnosed me with one of her fake fevers, and left me with a paracetamol.

I let myself be feverish for a few days.

v

Bonnie and Clyde

25

Following the wedding, Appa began to spend more time at work with Veronica Mannequin, going so far as to sleep at the shop several nights in a row. Amma wanted to resume her tuition classes but was worried students would make fun of her or, worse, that their parents, most of whom were in some way connected to Blue Hills, wouldn't send them to her in the first place. Instead she called schools and tried to find a full-time position teaching physics, maths or economics.

A week after the wedding, Sree and Anita moved into their new apartment. It was a one-bedroom on the windy seventh floor of a building complex called 'Elite'. I was still claiming feverishness but went there a couple of days later with Appa and Amma. We were on a mission to deliver some of Sree's clothes. The floor was marble and all the switchboards and fittings were new. It came fully furnished and the balcony overlooked a pocky cricket field.

The place was an uncanny dollhouse. The furniture was perfect, the walls were spotless – it was like a race of superior beings had abducted Sree and Anita and put them in their understanding of a human habitat. I touched the bananas to see if they were plastic, recalling, as I did, Anita's thing about aliens.

It was July now and the real monsoon had set in. It felt like eight or nine months had gone by instead of four or five. At that point, no one knew how to act any more. There was still plenty of anger on Appa and Amma's side. But they were also desperate to move forward. Problem was, none of us knew where we were going or how to get there.

Checking on Sreenath was part of Operation Bygones. While Appa hadn't wanted to come at all, Amma had been persistent. She'd been persistent with me too, citing the bags that needed to be carried upstairs and Appa's shoulder. Anyway, I was finding it hard to extricate myself now and stop feeling guilty.

The visit was unannounced. Anita stayed in the bedroom with the door locked. After Amma said something about the clothes to Sreenath and he mumbled back about where to put them – 'anywhere' – all of us acted as though we were real-estate customers thinking of buying the same apartment. We touched the walls, inspected the woodwork, tested the knobs.

'Must be quite expensive,' Appa said. 'No doubt, the rent is ridiculous too.'

He said this to me, not Sreenath. In Appa's head, reparative efforts probably had four levels: no talk in Sree's presence, small talk in Sree's presence, small talk about Sree in Sree's presence, and finally small talk with Sree.

Still on Level 2, Appa began explaining to me why the value of the apartment was likely to triple soon.

Amma wandered into the kitchen. A maid had been hired to cook, clean, and spy too, probably. I heard Amma advising her. The maid replied in Tamil and quickly grew annoyed.

Even more annoyed was Sreenath. We were there five minutes when he disappeared into the bathroom. He remained there for the rest of the visit. Appa's jaw relaxed once Sree left. He was certainly glad not to see Anita at all. Appa had confessed to finding her terrifying: the fact that she hadn't combusted even after so much.

'Pretty big screen,' he said, pointing to the TV in the hall. 'Must be sixty inches or so.'

I'm not sure if Anita's parents had visited them. At the very least, Mohan would have been dropping by every day to see how things were. He was the one who'd helped them move in the first place. Situations like these always brought out people like him.

This thought had just landed when I remembered Sree calling me a middleman. The idea that I had something in common with an oily fifty-year-old like Mohan made me leave the apartment and wait downstairs. I was still thinking about it in the car on our way back.

Appa said, 'That was a waste of time. Why should we go see him like he's royalty?'

Amma stared out of the window. 'How long will this continue?'

She asked this in the voice she usually reserved for God or the six p.m. news.

26

During their second week at the apartment, Anita posted pictures on Instagram. Most of them were screenshots from different articles – one about a by-election in Madhya Pradesh, another about Donald Trump, one about the Babri Masjid case – with captions that were excerpted from the articles themselves. They reiterated the same sort of opinions that most people in our circles held. To me their purpose seemed to be to say: 'I'm still here.'

Of the two non-screenshots she posted, one was a sketch of Sree sitting against the balcony door of their apartment. No real caption, just an ellipsis. The other was a more elaborate cartoon featuring a slim robot girl. A tiny human version of the same girl is shown sitting inside the robot version's head, piloting it. It had an esoteric caption. *The physical body is only a vessel. Nothing can get to you when you're in your head, looking out through the cockpit windows.*

Comments were always disabled. The post itself was deleted an hour after it went up.

Then one day, she set her account to private. Two days after that, I realised she'd blocked me and that Sreenath had deactivated his largely unused Facebook account.

The following week, he showed up at home. It was six in the evening. Amma had gone out to buy groceries and Appa, as usual, was at the shop. I didn't know Sree was coming over. When I opened the door, he acted like a proper guest.

'I just need to grab a few things,' he said. 'Can I do it now?'

'You don't have to ask me,' I said. 'This is your home too. Don't be so dramatic.'

After blowouts, no matter how big, we often talked like this. Like the person still sulking was making too much of what should have been forgotten long ago.

Sree didn't say anything. I'd rather he turned mad. I wanted to both punch him and be punched by him. I felt that if we punched each other just the right way, certain words would come tumbling out and everything would be all right.

Sree went upstairs. I followed him and tried to help.

Since Sree's exile, I'd made a point of going in and out of his room whenever I could. If I saw the door closed, I'd kick it open. If I wanted a pen or an empty notebook, I'd take one from his drawer. I did this so that it didn't become a sentimental shrine Appa and Amma might stare at as they passed by.

Sree packed in a hurry. It had started drizzling.

'Why do you want all this now?' I asked.

'It's not doing anything here.'

By the time he was done, he had two bags full of books, clothes and miscellaneous items including his mementoes – the coffee cups, the scrunchie, the watch dial.

'You don't want your magazines?'

'No.'

'The notebooks?'

'No.'

Underneath the bed there was a bottle of Black Dog. Sree and I had drunk some in secret during the previous New Year, standing at the window and watching an altercation between neighbours with great glee.

I wondered if there was a way to bring this up. Both of us on the same side, looking out.

The rain had become a thin sheet.

'I'll help you carry the bags,' I said. 'You won't get an auto.'

He wouldn't even let me walk him past the front step.

*

It was about thirty minutes after Sreenath left that I found his ATM card on the bed. I thought about it for a while then put on my raincoat, started the scooter, and rode over to Sree's apartment.

I arrived just as the rain grew out of control. I got stranded. Sree wasn't pleased, obviously. The ATM card was his old one too. But when I lingered by the door, refreshing the weather app, he didn't throw me out. I think this was because throwing me out would have required him to take some kind of ownership of the apartment. He simply left the door open and went away.

While Sree and Anita stayed in the bedroom, I sat in the hall, reading on my phone. Then the power went out.

Anita came into the living room, lit a cigarette and stared out at the balcony. Sree followed.

'Your building doesn't have a generator?' I asked.

Nobody answered and it remained dark, so, 'Clearly not,' I said.

Next question, 'Have you guys had dinner? Anita?'

She took several puffs of the cigarette. 'Yup.'

'Right. You guys have the maid. She is Tamilian, yes?'

Anita didn't answer. To be honest, I'd annoyed even myself.

A minute later, there was a knock. Sree went to open the door and held it closed behind him. I understood from the conversation that it was Joel delivering pot.

'We are good,' I heard Sree say. 'Just riding it out for now. You know how it is.'

He didn't invite Joel inside.

I asked Anita, 'Did your friends say anything about the marriage?'

I said the word 'marriage' quietly.

Anita stubbed her cigarette, lit another one, shrugged.

Once Joel left, Sree returned to the living room holding a slim baggie of brown-green fuzz. 'People are going about,' he told me. 'It's not raining so much.'

I hesitated and stood up. It occurred to me that the real reason I'd stuck around was to say something apologetic. I sighed.

'It's horrible the way everything turned out. But given the

circumstances it could have gone a lot worse. I'm sorry if I said some things that were hurtful or ill-conceived.'

Sree had his finger in the baggie and was examining the composition of its contents.

'Sure,' he finally said. 'Take care.'

I waited for something else. 'This is pretty messed up, though,' I said. 'Especially as the dust settles. I agree a hundred per cent with you on that and I know *you know* I agree.'

Sree said, 'What's done is done.'

I should have left it at that. That was a good response.

But because it was good, almost too good to believe in and end on, I found myself saying, 'The other day I was looking up some things online. Maybe you guys should see a therapist. Just talk it all out. Eventually maybe everyone together. I don't know how else anybody will ever get back to normal. I was talking about it to –'

'Oh just fuck off already,' Sree said. 'I fucking hate the sight of your face. I really do.'

Suddenly I was angry as well. 'If you want to hate someone, hate her mother,' I said, pointing to Anita. 'I didn't want to get involved in any of this. I was minding my own business. You weren't home so you don't know how bad it was. You left me to superglue the pieces.'

Sree put the baggie on the teapoy.

I said, 'And I agree this is horrible, but it just happened to be a pragmatic truce.'

Sree said, 'Right. As we have seen before.'

I felt he was talking about the engineering mess.

'Grow up,' I said. 'It's not like anyone is out here *trying* to wreck your life.'

'Yeah, kicking me out when I most needed help was very excellent.'

'You could have handled that way better. I know you were under stress, but you could have handled it way better.'

'Because they handled it perfectly.'

'No. And I told them the same thing I'm telling you.'

'Oh you *did*. That's *so* nice of you. That's so lovely.'

Before I could reply, Sree said, 'Nice chatting. I'll call you again when there's an emergency. Or when one of my friends needs a pig breathing down on them and masturbating to their photos.'

If I weren't so brown, I would have turned red. Was this Sree's take or had Dhruti said something to him? Aside from asking her for coffee and then rudely hanging up, a few days back, I had accidentally liked an old beach photo of hers on Instagram and then immediately unliked it. I'd also called her one night. This was to clear the air. Dhruti hadn't picked up or called back. I'd then left a text saying, *Hey, you still up for that coffee?* to which she'd replied, *I'll let you know* :). Needless to say, she hadn't let me know, and I'd been thinking about it since.

'Sure, I'm the pig,' I said. 'Why don't you cover yourself in mud and screw right by the front gate?'

Anita said, 'Will you please just leave?'

Sree took off his slipper and boomeranged it casually in my direction, like he was, in fact, aiming to park it by the door. I dodged, walked out and kept walking.

I did try and talk to Sree once more after that, but only because I had something practical to say.

Several copies of the video were still online. I wasn't exactly keeping tabs but I occasionally checked the links to see if any had been removed. I think new copies might have been popping up as well. In any case, they got a lot of views, as many as 400,000. Most came with comment sections where people asked if there were more videos of the same couple, or called Sree ugly or stupid or irresponsible. There were lots of comments about his penis size too.

With Anita, people complimented her looks – though maybe compliment is not the word – while also calling her dumb and unfortunate. These were just the comments in English. I couldn't really understand the Hindi stuff.

One evening, I noticed a comment that mentioned Sree and

Anita by their full names along with the name of their college. It was in reply to someone who'd asked: *Know who they are? Is there a longer version?* That's when I texted Sree. The video was on one of the big sites. I think he must have managed to flag it. It was soon marked for review.

Sree didn't respond to my messages.

27

When Sreenath and Anita left Trivandrum a few weeks later, I was fast asleep. Their doorman saw the elevator descend sometime between three and four a.m. He'd been awake studying for the Civil Services exam. Sree and Anita were carrying a suitcase each, both bulky, and gave the doorman a salute.

They'd always been nice to him. Nearly every middle-of-the-night the past two weeks, they'd been going on walks and always they'd stopped by to say hello. They would also borrow his baton to fence off any street dogs. It was only for thirty or forty minutes, so he let them take it.

Coming back, Sree and Anita would often have something in their hands. Bits of movie posters torn from walls – Mohanlal's head, for instance. Or a bunch of election banners. One time they'd somehow managed to unscrew and bring home a metal NO PARKING sign. They never took anything from, or damaged, the premises of the building complex, so it wasn't the doorman's business what they did.

Also not his business: to ask tenants where they were going when they went out with suitcases. But Sree had volunteered and said, 'Honeymoon.' Anita had said, 'Good luck for your exams. Don't forget, Khasi is the main language of Meghalaya, not Mizoram.'

They weren't cheerful, though, no. If anything they seemed sadder than usual.

It was a cold morning. A car was waiting with maybe two people inside. It wasn't a taxi. Not a blue Santro either. It might have been a small SUV. The doorman heard the group talking. Then the car left and he went back to his books.

Mohan was meditating when he got a call from Anita. It was nine a.m. She told him they had left town and did not want to be contacted ever again. No questions were answered. Mohan then sent someone to the apartment. Sree and Anita's personal items were gone save for some clothes and books. In their bedroom cupboard, there were rusty signs and dozens of random posters.

Mohan called Amma. Amma couldn't understand what he was saying because of the poor connection. She gave the phone to me.

It was a Thursday and I'd just returned from a quick run along the beach.

Mohan talked for twenty minutes.

It's true that I had found it difficult to picture Sree and Anita living in that apartment for long, but I hadn't expected them to just pack up and go away either. I'd predicted there would be more fights, maybe a sit-down. After all, they hadn't run away *before* the wedding despite Sree bringing it up. Why would they want to put themselves through more discomfort now? Wasn't it better simply to be in a controlled environment?

Once the call was over, I kept the phone pressed against my ear. I remembered Sree coming home to pick up his things and felt stupid. Had our last conversation then really been our last conversation?

When I told the news to Amma, I did so hoping it wouldn't become another *Hindenburg*. And maybe because of our recent conditioning, the effect really was numbed.

Amma seemed irritated. The way she would be if the electrician had promised to come and then hadn't. She sat down on the sofa, scratched her face, and asked me if I could call Sreenath. I knew it was pointless. Sure enough, both their phones were unreachable. There weren't any traces of them online either.

'Check with his friends, then.'

She rattled off three or four names that she'd heard around the house. I rang Joel who said he didn't know of any plans, very sorry. He sounded that way too. I texted Meghna as well but not Dhruti or Arjun.

When Appa found out, he tried to act nonchalant but ended up angry.

'If they want to vanish, let them,' he said. 'But when they ruin their lives and come knocking on our door, it will remain tightly shut. No question about that.'

I imagined Sree and Anita driving away from the city.

In reality it could have been that they were carsick somewhere, worried about the future, wishing they could sleep in a comfortable bed. My mind had them going top down, top speed, blasting Brigitte Bardot's 'Bonnie and Clyde', attacking signboards and graffitiing walls.

The rest of us were far behind, coughing in a funny cloud of dust.

That was on the first day.

By Day Three and Four, emotions in the house ran high. Anxiety about next steps, sudden concerns over Sree's safety and health. Appa and Amma began bashing Anita's mother.

'You can't just rush into such things and not expect consequences,' Amma said.

Appa said maybe *he* should drive over, park in *her* porch and wait inside till *she* solved this.

How Anita's mother would react was a worry, though. She called us before the end of the week.

This wasn't the first time she'd called. Several days after the wedding, she'd rung Amma saying a friend of hers was starting a primary school, would Amma be willing to consult? Amma had said she'd think about it.

Anita's mother had then gone on to complain about migraines and blackouts. 'I've been having them for quite a while now,' she'd said. 'When the pain overwhelms you, you can think of nothing else. You become a different person. Yesterday I ate two breakfasts. The second one I only ate because I completely forgot I'd even had the first one.'

'Right,' Amma said, sceptical.

'It can be quite frightening. The absolute loss of control.'

But with Anita's mother sounding embarrassed, Amma was filled with indignation. She'd hung up saying she had some work and never called back.

This time, too, Anita's mother seemed softer, eager to avoid a fuss. 'We have done our duty and can relax knowing this,' she said. 'That's the important thing. Everything else is in their hands.' Then, after delivering a piece about trying to track them down anyway and maybe even dispatching Mohan on an all-India tour, she casually added, 'For now, I'm telling everybody that they are in Chennai. I think you should probably do that as well. It's better than letting all sorts of rumours spread again.'

Amma wasn't openly hostile to her, but as soon as the call ended, she began talking about how Anita's mother cared only about her family's image. I said, 'Yes, it's good that we are so different.'

Appa said, 'It's even better that you have joined us to offer your witty remarks.'

I left the living room and went upstairs.

One thing that didn't surprise me any more was that the sun rose no matter what happened to us. And because no one had reacted substantially to Sree's leaving, it felt like the days were going by too fast.

In the beginning, there was talk of them coming back in a month or so. 'They must be somewhere around here.' Amma said this every now and then, like Sree was an item we'd misplaced, bound eventually to turn up under the sofa or in a random cupboard.

The apartment was left on rent. Occasionally Anita's side

would ask if Sree had tried to contact us, especially me. I ended up answering calls from every internet provider, insurance agency and fraudster in India.

The residents of Blue Hills, at least Amma's friends, already knew about the wedding. The soft-boiled and warped version Amma had spooned them, that is. By the time two or three weeks had passed, she started leaking that Sreenath had moved to another city. Word spread that he had in fact run away.

People began showing us sympathy. Murthi uncle from No. 18 suggested to Appa that Appa and I climb Sabarimala on our bare feet. He himself had done so recently and it had been transformative. Appa said, 'Yes, you have lost weight. Good.'

Ramesh uncle from Downing Street presented Appa with a statue of the Laughing Buddha. For good luck. Appa felt that the Buddha was in fact laughing *at* him. What was so funny and why was he so fat? Appa put it deep inside the bedroom cupboard.

Whenever I ran into Amma's friends now, they took me aside and told me that I had to support my parents and do my best to be a good son. I heard both these things on a daily basis.

With me standing there, Aunty 1 would say to Aunty 2, 'He's actually very focused. He can really pull off something amazing. You know he was a rank-holder for most of university?' That wasn't true – I had held rank for one semester, and that too, barely. I figured they said it because it highlighted the Sreenath mess more. Perhaps it also made them feel better about themselves.

Those days saw frequent power cuts. The ones that came at night were especially depressing. Sitting in my room felt like being in a cave. Sometimes Amma would say, 'At least we still have you.'

In response, I tried ignoring her and Appa as much as possible.

Once again, I stopped eating at home. I turned down even the simplest requests, like watering the plants or buying groceries. I certainly wasn't going to soap Appa in the shower.

Given the circumstances, he felt I should remain close. Get a job in the city itself, or if not that, then go help him at the shop for a while.

One day he dumped a load of MBA books on my desk.

'If you study well, you can get into an IIM,' he said.

I shouted at him, saying I needed time to calm down after all the nonsense they'd put me through. Normally, Appa wasn't the type to tolerate this sort of behaviour. He would have lined up some interview, stapled a tie on me, and dragged me to it by surprise. He would have grilled me about my future and made jokes about attending my poetry recital.

A job in the city was the last thing I wanted. I was already applying to several positions that would take me far out of the state. But Appa's request that I stick around made me second-guess everything. I skipped scheduled interviews. I continued ignoring mails that showed an interest in my CV. Instead, I sat around checking bus and train times and hotel rates across the country.

I realised I was waiting for some signal that we had reached a permanent future. This waiting made time feel useless for anything except to get us from where we were to somewhere more decisive.

Sree had been gone two months when I ran into an acquaintance of his at the supermarket. The acquaintance didn't recognise me as Sree's brother, only as someone he'd seen in his company.

He told me that Sree and Anita seemed to be shuffling from place to place, and might have been too shy to show their faces. *Yet*, there had been sightings. Somebody reported that they looked gaunt. One rumour said Sree was an alcoholic. Another had them working in Dubai.

'I mean, it's gotta be one of the top twenty-five home-made *Indian* videos in a while,' the acquaintance said. 'If there's an Oscars for pornography, and you know what, *actually*, I think there *is* one. In California. And it's called –'

In his shopping trolley was a carton of eggs. While I had the childish urge to break a few over his head, I'd also been carrying with me, for a while now, a dim awareness that I'd watched many such videos myself over the past many years on many bored explorations across many sites without asking too many questions.

The fancier egg cartons, in one of the other aisles I'd just walked through, had yellow packaging that said: *Do you know where your eggs come from?*

The one in his trolley just said: *24 fresh eggs.*

When I looked up, the acquaintance was asking me questions. Where did I think Sree and Anita were? Had anyone else heard from them?

I told him I had no idea. He seemed disappointed.

Sometime in November, I saw Appa showing Amma an article that had appeared in the *Mathrubhumi*. It was about honour killings. He saw me and said, 'You also. Come here and check what it says.' The article talked about an incident in Uttar Pradesh. A 23-year-old engineering student and the girl he loved were stabbed twelve times and then burned with acid by the girl's relatives.

'This is what some people do,' Appa said happily. 'And they do it for a lot less. A whole lot less.'

Three months had gone by. I'd decided to train for a local marathon and was running every day till the world was covered in spots. We didn't really discuss Sreenath. I didn't check in with any of his friends. Not Joel, Arjun, Meghna, and not Dhruti, who, maybe on Sree's instruction, had blocked me on Instagram. Often I would find myself wondering about him. Which state. Which city. What kind of house. What kind of people.

I saw this glazed look pass over Appa's and Amma's faces too. There were also times when I thought, Good riddance.

On Karthika aunty's recommendation, Amma had subscribed to Netflix. This was so she could keep herself distracted. She hardly watched it. Appa said, 'Everywhere you look, there's nothing but garbage.'

28

Once when Sree was fourteen, he told Appa that he wanted to attend a residential camp that our school was conducting in Ernakulam. All his friends were going. The brochure had pictures of people like Abdul Kalam, Azim Premji and Sachin Tendulkar. The camp would focus on personality development and physical education, but the general idea was: join us and become a part of the Great Indian Success Story.

Appa and Amma fell in love with it. Sree hadn't really stayed away before, not for long anyway. The camp would last six days. On the week that he was due to leave, it was hot and sunny, and the clear light made even small spaces appear vast.

I remember a moment, after Sree and Appa had got in the car and left for the train station, when I exhaled fully and deflated on the verandah. It was a Sunday evening. This was back in the old house. The streets were quiet and I could hear a neighbour in his bathroom, ferociously throwing water on himself. A group of children were going home after tuition. They clopped along with heavy bags, shading their eyes.

I was still sitting on the verandah when, thirty minutes later, Appa came back with Sree in the passenger seat.

I jumped up and yelled, 'Appa didn't drop him off.'

Amma came out. What happened was that, while waiting on the platform, Sree had told Appa that he had an odd feeling about the whole thing. Nothing specific, just an odd feeling. A bad odd feeling. Usually Appa detested people who changed their minds. This time, though, just as the train crawled up, he'd put Sree in the car and brought him back home. Appa told Amma, 'It's good that he spoke up. Sometimes you have to trust your gut. Who knows how these things work.' The universe, he meant.

As Sree unpacked, I asked him, 'Did you really have a premonition?'

'I didn't say I had a premonition,' he said. 'I said I had a *feeling*.'

'What kind of a *feeling*?' I was making fun of him.

So he acted even more serious. 'Just that, if I left, I might not make it home ever again.' He looked at the floor. 'It was this intense need to get back. Sit here. Just be here.'

The wind had picked up. In the kitchen, Amma was making tea. Everyone seemed unreasonably happy and the whole evening had a comforting and mysterious tightness – even if it only lasted for a short time.

Project12's
Kafkaaaa

29

Sometimes I imagined running into Sree at a supermarket in the far future. In this scenario, I'm successful and married. Sree is still with Anita and they are substantially poorer than me; I can tell from their clothes and the way they take each item off the shelf and study it for a long time before putting it in their cart. I ask Sree to have a coffee with me. At first he refuses, but soon enough, we sit down and talk and reach some kind of an understanding. Sensing that his money troubles are deep, I offer to help him out. *What's mine is yours*, I say. He calls me corny. This must be happening somewhere foreign because snow starts falling outside the big coffee-shop window. We warm our hands over our mugs and watch the white puffs settle on the street.

In another scenario, I imagined Sree coming home a year later. When I open the door, he goes upstairs to his room without saying a word. It takes a while, but eventually we all have dinner together. Since it can't snow, it rains.

The third scenario wasn't pleasant but sometimes it seemed most likely. In this, Sree and Anita kill themselves. We find out from the police. I refuse to let Appa, Amma or Anita's parents attend the funeral. Afterwards, I don't talk to anyone and disappear to another country, possibly one where it snows.

In real life, nothing happened for over five months after Sree left home. No news reached us. The video continued to remain online. The quiet felt unnatural, as though our problems had been squeezed down into uneasy and ill-fitting nooks, where they were waiting to spring out and surprise us at any moment.

It was January. I was at my desk working on sums for a mock CAT exam – which I'd decided to sit after all – while also looking for MBA coaching centres outside the state, checking Instagram, and browsing Facebook on my laptop. I was about to log out when I saw it. There was a point when I scrolled past the video, did an almost comical double take, and scrolled back up at full speed.

The first thing I noticed was the band's name, Project12. This itself didn't turn the light bulb on. That only happened when I looked at the page's profile picture and remembered seeing the singer and her bassist at Sree's place. My eyes hurt from squinting. I waited for a few seconds, read the comments to give myself some context, then clicked on the video. It buffered and began playing at full volume. I scrambled to find my headphones.

Maybe the following description is unnecessary, but I'll say it anyway. The video had been trimmed from its original twelve minutes to just under five – that's how long the song was. The more salacious bits had either been removed or covered with silly animated characters – a bald uncle, a fat aunty in a saree, a crowd of people – all of which, I realised right away, had been drawn by Anita. The music was techno. This was accompanied by wispy vocals that talked about a lot of nothing: finding yourself transformed and I don't know what else. To those who didn't know about the original cut, the video might have seemed more or less normal, or at least on par with the strange way music videos are often shot. The song was titled 'Kafkaaaa'. Maybe because I'm biased, everything about it sounded juvenile.

The video had been uploaded to YouTube and Vimeo about five days previously. The YouTube description credited 'two amazing people' with 'special thanks for doing this and being enviably, unimpeachably cool'. The Facebook share that I saw had over two thousand likes. I couldn't stop chewing on my fingers.

It was hotter than usual that Sunday afternoon. When I went downstairs at lunch, Appa and Amma were sipping Tang and watching TV. I must have looked confused because they asked if everything was all right. I said yes.

By the time I returned to my room, the YouTube view count had jumped from around 50,000 to 50,200. I watched a part of the video again, reread the song's description, checked some more comments, and tried to find Sree or Anita online. I felt I had a vague idea of what they were trying to do but not what it meant for the rest of us.

The next several hours, I sat in front of the laptop, feeling nauseated at the smell of overheated plastic. I considered deleting my Facebook account and acting as though this entire thing was taking place in a different dimension. When I went to sleep, the YouTube version had 51,000 views and I was refreshing it every two minutes.

I didn't tell Appa and Amma. They only found out four days later, when the video had crossed 100,000 views and Appa's brother called.

Appa couldn't understand what was going on. His response on the phone had been: 'Yes, the video is in a few places. What can you do.' By 'video', he meant the original thing.

'That's not the one I'm talking about,' Appa's brother said.

Then Appa made me explain to him the concept of this music video, where exactly it was being watched, and how many people were watching it. I told him as best I could, but made sure to downplay it.

'It's just a stupid art thing,' I said. 'No one will care.'

'Why do they have insects all over them?'

'I don't know. Because of Franz Kafka. He's a writer, Appa. He's dead and used to –'

Appa shouted, 'I know who he is. Don't patronise me all the time. You think I'm an idiot?'

The chances of Appa knowing Kafka were about as high as Kafka knowing him. He looked wounded, though.

Amma asked, 'But you're saying these people used the video with Sreenath's permission?'

'Probably. But I don't think it matters. This will die down in a second.'

At that point, both Appa and Amma had made peace with the video remaining online forever. None of us, however, had anticipated this sort of renewed attention. I can imagine how puzzled they must have been. After spending the better part of a year talking about getting it removed, here it was online again, this time remixed to a weird song and even weirder animation. I'm surprised their heads didn't fall off.

Over the coming days, Amma took it upon herself to torture the shop's books and cut expenses. She sat hunched at the dining table with a magnifying glass. Appa worked late and managed to tire himself out so he had no choice but to sleep as soon as he came home.

While I didn't see any of Sree's university friends sharing the video, plenty of random people did. Those who had seen it in its pornographic form must have found this new incarnation especially amusing. On YouTube, the view count crossed 150K. A friend from school messaged me asking if I knew what was up.

On the Wednesday that it reached 200,000, Anita's mother called us for an explanation. It was morning and Appa was running around trying to find his expensive watch. He was wearing it everywhere now.

No sooner had he answered the phone than there was an argument. 'We should be asking *you* how to fix this,' Appa said. 'You took charge of the situation when you married them off, and first they run away and now this. *You* should be the one figuring this out.'

She hung up before Appa could say that thing about sitting in his car in front of her house. He then started fighting with Amma about how he was the one who had to keep dealing with Anita's mother. One of them broke a plate. It's a miracle really that we don't all just eat off the floor at my house.

30

When I'd downplayed the video to Appa before, I hadn't exactly been *downplaying* it. My first estimate really had been that nothing much would happen. The band wasn't famous. The video would make the rounds for a few days and then get dumped like everything else. I figured the internet was already too full and that another distraction wasn't going to stick.

But the following week, a popular newspaper's blog carried an article about the music video, describing it as an 'interesting phenomenon'. The day after that I saw another piece. This one was about two hundred words and included a screenshot. Also included were names and quotes, making that the first time we were hearing from Sreenath or Anita in over five months.

Sreenath said, *More and more people were seeing it anyway, so when Project approached us, we thought this would be a good way of saying: we are fine with it. In a sense, it was about taking control of the narrative and putting it behind us.* Anita was quoted saying, *We also thought it would be interesting to flip the context and transform it into something else altogether.*

I felt Sree and Anita were unreal entities, already very far away. I remembered the sign-tearing and the poster-pulling. I also thought: Who do they think they are?

I now feel that neither of them had intended for the music video to be a sensation. They'd likely assumed that it would get a few views and bounce around among friends who'd find it clever and novel and brave. In the scheme of things, they must have thought, it wouldn't matter – a worse version of it was online already.

Maybe then they got carried away or were egged on.

Afterwards I left home and went to a coffee shop. I opened the article again and double-checked to see if it mentioned Sreenath and Anita's location. I then scrolled through Facebook and saw that a few of Sree's friends and several strangers had shared it. A random NRI woman from Texas had called them courageous. Somebody from Bhopal had commented on it with a row of clap emojis.

Two days later, there was a third article. This one featured Nisha, the singer of the band. Nisha talked about how she had known the couple for a while, how impressed she had been by their attitude, how the idea of the video had started off as a joke, and how she'd approached them once again when they had run into each other.

All this further compounded Appa and Amma's incomprehension.

Amma, reading the article over and over again, said: 'Don't people have anything else to care about? Why are we being cursed like this?'

Appa, to me: 'Is this his way of getting revenge?'

Nisha: *You have to seize your moment and make your statement. Haters can stfu.*

31

I didn't think my plan for that evening would be any different from my plan for all other evenings: sit at my desk, try to solve sample papers, insert food into my mouth, listen to my parents, surf the net, lie down, bide my time. I was in the lying-down phase when my bed started to vibrate and wouldn't stop. Downstairs, Appa and Amma were arguing. I checked my phone. While I didn't recognise the number, I could see the WhatsApp profile picture. Mohan was standing against a white column with his arms crossed. A large phone leaned over the balcony of his shirt pocket. He was grinning. His status read: *Never say NO, never say, 'I cannot', for you are INFINITE. All the power is WITHIN you. You can do anything – Swami Vivekananda.*

A message followed asking me if I could please call him back for an urgent discussion.

I suppose this was when something cleared the block between thought and action. In my head now, it's all very fluid.

I got up. I knew exactly which bag I wanted to take and must have been ogling it for months by then. I packed four shirts, two pairs of jeans, a ball of underwear, some socks, my laptop and a bit of money I'd saved. I also knew the bus and train times by heart. I checked the ticket prices on my phone.

The guy with whom I'd had my 'significant experience' back in college, his name was Rishi. Neither of us were good at keeping in touch, but occasionally we'd exchange news articles that annoyed us. Once I decided on Bangalore – the closest big city – he was the first person I thought of. Rishi had moved there after finishing his BA at Delhi University and now lived with his boyfriend. I called him and asked if I could stay a few days. He seemed puzzled for a moment. Then his casa, he said, was my casa.

I have acted on impulse maybe seven times in my life, including the Dhruti incident of not long ago and a faecal incident in class three. That night makes it seven and a half or, okay, eight. Between my deciding to do it and doing it, less than two hours must have passed.

All of a sudden I was standing in the living room with my bag. Appa and Amma were at the dining table. They were frowning at something on Appa's computer.

'I have an urgent job interview,' I said. My throat felt dry.

Appa looked up. 'What job interview?' I noticed him taking in the bag and the fact that I was dressed. I'd even made a point of wearing shoes.

'I already told you a few days back. It's in Bangalore. You don't listen.'

Appa and Amma blinked. I threw my hands up.

'The ticket is already booked,' I said. Like it was common knowledge you went to jail if you didn't honour your ticket.

Appa started talking about how I was being stupid. I should be focusing on the MBA entrance instead of attending random job interviews, and that too across state lines. Amma also joined in.

'I'll let you know once it's done,' I said. 'I'm not sure how long it'll take.'

'How can you just leave?' Appa said. 'In the middle of all this.'

I stood there for a few seconds thinking about this middle and shifting the weight of the bag from one hand to the other. The living room was dark. The fan was turned up to five. It wasn't that hot and still I was covered in sweat.

'The range is bad when the network is roaming,' I said. 'But I'll message once I get there.'

'Absolutely not,' Appa said.

I was already shuffling backwards to the door. I opened it.

Appa didn't give chase and neither did Amma. They just stood there. Appa holding a pen. Amma with her mouth slightly open. I was out the door, out of Blue Hills, in an auto. I kept looking back. Still no chase. I kept patting my pockets too. Wallet, phone. Wallet, phone. Wallet, phone. I had the sense that I had forgotten something important or that I needed something more to go on a trip like this.

Later, in the bus, I listened to music at full volume – as you are supposed to do, I thought, in situations like this. I received missed calls from Appa and Amma. One, three, five. Six by the time we left city limits. Nine by the time the bus was at a rest stop. Four hours had gone by since I left home. I felt excellent, full of energy. It was midnight and I almost howled.

The rest stop consisted of a parking lot and a line of bathrooms. Crazy insects were moshing around large white lights. My departure had happened so fast that I barely knew where I was. I took a deep breath. The air smelled of concentrated urine but I gulped it down anyway. I even opened the text app on my phone and wrote: *The night was cold and my lungs were full.* I nodded to the other passengers who were standing around by the wild grass. Most were only a few years older than me. When they nodded back, I felt buoyant. Then I went around borrowing cigarettes. I didn't even want to smoke them.

Back on the speeding bus, I logged into Facebook and messaged about two dozen Bangalore-based acquaintances saying I was in the city. One replied right away with, *So?* But even that couldn't bring me down.

For the rest of the night, I thought about what I might do next. Get a job. If not in journalism, then in advertising. Maybe I could find Piyush Pandey and mention late Father Pauli's offer. I could find a way to write films or direct plays. I could go to medical school, become a doctor. Heart. Liver. Kidney. A goddamn penis surgeon. No one could stop me. I could find a flat. Buy new clothes. Change my hairstyle. Join a gym. Get a girlfriend. *Buy* a flat. *Marry* my girlfriend. Start my own family. Be a millionaire.

175

It occurred to me that taglines weren't just lies. The impossible really was nothing. I could *just do it*. Outside, we were churning scenery, overtaking everything. I could have sworn I felt the wind through the sealed windows. My teeth chattered.

Even without adrenaline, Bangalore carried weight. I pictured shopping malls you could camp in, and people walking all around the city, going club to club, house party to house party till early morning. Then they'd stumble into their colourful offices, nursing icepacks and talking about how watermelons cured hangovers.

If I slept, it was only for a second each time. My vision was liquid.

By morning, I was fourteen missed calls away from home. Seven hundred kilometres had gone by. I saw an arrow of fluorescent joggers in Nike tracks. The bus was pulling into Madiwala station.

32

I might have thought about Sreenath once or twice before I booked my bus ticket – Malayalis tended to collect in Bangalore and it did occur to me that Sree's being there wasn't a bad bet – but beyond that, it wasn't as though I was expecting to meet him. In fact, I was sincerely focusing all my energy on self-propulsion.

The more condensed version of what then happened is this:

As I set off to Rishi's apartment, the morning felt nutritious. With the momentum I had, I could have gone anywhere. I could have got out of my taxi and run to Tibet. I could have freed it too. The sun was up but everything was cool. The roads were wet and, even though it was only eight, already busy. Above the traffic at one junction, a metro train went screeching by. I saw two girls in jean shorts standing on the pavement and feeding a polite circle of dogs. Back home, you would have been hard-pressed to find girls in shorts. They would have been leered to death. Already it felt like I was entering a kinder, more generous place.

Rishi and his boyfriend, Shashank, lived in an apartment in leafy Indiranagar. I hadn't met Shashank before but on Instagram they looked identical in graphic Ts and heavy beards. They were settled: TV, bookshelf, sofa. A newspaper lay open on the teapoy. Next to it on the floor was a plate of half-eaten sandwiches. The dining table was made of dark wood. They'd set out a fruit bowl with a few oranges and apples. They even had one of those novelty salt and pepper shakers, shaped like ducks.

If I were to walk into a furniture store and see this exact same tableau, sandwiches and all, even now I would go broke.

It was a Saturday but Shashank had left for work and Rishi was alone. Both of them worked for think-tanks. One dealt with land allocation, the other with potable water.

I said, 'And what do you get when you combine your powers?' This was the kind of mood I was in. Looking back, I can see that I might have been manic. I was aware that all these other things were happening in the background, that I'd left home abruptly with nothing more than vague ideas, that I had a phone accruing missed calls, that there was something bad turning worse, but I was also set on following what seemed like a forward trajectory.

My first hour there, I brushed my teeth, then lied through them. One reason I'd wanted to stay with Rishi was because he didn't know about the video and I wouldn't have to get into it. Rishi didn't like the home crowd. They were too daft for his taste. He had his posh Delhi University crowd and his Bangalore crowd and that was it.

I told him that, aside from looking for a job, I was there to research a non-fiction book. I then started describing it based on a plot I'd thought up for a university assignment. It involved the Travancore royal family, a murder and the treasures in Pad-manabhaswamy Temple.

Rishi said, 'Sounds interesting. Like that guy, what's his name, the journalist who wrote *Killers of the Flower Moon*?'

'David Grann.'

Getting this name right gave me such joy, such a feeling of success, that I grinned widely and Rishi asked me if there was some joke he was missing.

I'm normally not a liar but other lies started coming out. Thinking of Dhruti, I told him I was in an on-off relationship with this girl back home, 'a weeb'. 'A few months back, though, we finally decided not to see each other for good.' And this had been hard. It had taken a toll on 'my work'. I'd been drinking too much.

At various points as I went on bragging, I did wonder if Rishi knew about Sreenath and wasn't telling me. Then I wondered if, at the end of the day, we were insignificant after all, if everything had just seemed magnified when in reality it was a small nothing with caterpillar legs and no mileage.

This last thought was so relieving that it literally cleared my nose. More light rushed in. My eyes started beaming.

'What?' Rishi said, staring at me. 'Are you high?'

'Do you have pot?'

The two of us got coffee; my sixth in a row including all the coffees I'd drunk roadside. I talked about the movies I'd seen recently. 'You should check out this Marathi one, *Court*. Great stuff' and 'You haven't seen *Kumbalangi Nights* yet? Is this a rock, Rishi? Are we under a rock right now?' The fact that I hadn't watched even a single Terrence Malick movie didn't stop me from saying, 'Honestly, how are people *still* discussing Terrence Malick? He can Malick my balls.' I kept score. I lied and said I'd finished second in my university. I said, 'Were you guys not able to torrent at DU? How could you possibly miss *Your Name*? I thought DU folk were supposed to be cream of the nerd crop. And *Your Name* isn't even nerdy. It's straight up mainstream.' Then I moved on to books. I said it was better these days to claim you *hadn't* read *Infinite Jest* than to say you had. I'd found this opinion online. '*Pale King* is superior,' I said. 'You can really see why he killed himself.'

Rishi was reserved. It's entirely possible that he was scared for his life. Here was a guy who'd barged into his home, eyes open just a bit too wide, energy of a peak-performing aerobics instructor, continuously raving about a hundred things, cackling and cracking jokes at an incredible rate, berating his friend's alma mater some two dozen times in ten sentences, pulling his phone out and shoving it back into his pocket again and again and again.

Maybe Rishi thought I was on the lam for murder.

But he was not an uncouth person. He listened politely and even joined in with an anecdote about some exhibition. I quickly invented my own exhibition anecdote.

Rishi asked, 'On a scale of one to Trivandrum, how bad is Trivandrum now?'

'Trivandrum,' I said. 'They talk about how you've gone full-blown homosexual, by the way.'

'Never changes, that place.'

'Goddamn homophobes everywhere, you won't believe it.'

That was exaggeration, but trashing the city put Rishi in gear. We ended up berating the place so much that I came close to telling him about the mess at home. *Get this* – I imagined myself saying. Or *You want an idea of how fucked up things really are? Listen to this.*

In the early afternoon, Amma sent me a link. I decided to ignore it. The previous message in our chat had been from me to her. For the sake of my conscience, just: *Reached. All good.*

An hour went by and she spammed me the same thing four times. I paced the apartment, asked Rishi about the job market, gave him advice on getting a good job, tried to play his PS4. The phone in my pocket started to feel heavy and my earlier buoyancy faded. While Rishi was on a call, I went to the bathroom and checked the message.

Till now, none of the articles had gone into much depth about Sree or Anita. This one was longer, about six hundred words. It was in a major national newspaper's supplement. I read it twice. It was much worse than the others.

If I had to give an exact turning point within the article, I'd say it was when Sree was asked about people's initial reaction. Something must have tripped in his head because he went on a tirade. He called the Indian culture prudish and prissy. He said that most Indians were repressed; that India was just stuck-up and backward; that the majority of the older generation needed a moral realignment.

My parents kicked me out of the house when they found out about the video, he said. *My father actually slapped me and threw my birth certificate at me. Then Anita's parents got involved, and believe it or not, a few weeks later, we were being forced to get married.*

Anita's response was similar, perhaps less emphatic.

I imagined Sree sitting in front of the interviewer, sweating too much, sipping their bad coffee, and ranting more than he had intended to. I also imagined him speaking with conviction, saying exactly what he wanted.

The article had come out the previous afternoon, but it was late at night that a progressive MP from Kerala shared it on Facebook. He'd quoted the bit about the parents and the marriage with the caption, *Remind me which century we live in again?*

I sat on the toilet and scrolled down to see the huge stack of comments and shares. The older ones criticised regressiveness: there were so many, my phone froze as they loaded.

Then some of the other things said by Sree and Anita seemed to catch people's eye. A couple of comments called them snooty. A few others called them attention seekers and drama queens. I think that's how they began to get it too.

The most-liked comment on the MP's post now said, *You were caught jerking it in the bushes. Why are you being all philosophical about this, buddy? LOL.*

I clicked on the guy's profile. He was a medical student from Ernakulam.

In another top comment, a 35-year-old woman, someone who posted a lot of dieting-related content, said: *There's this great new invention. It comes with 'walls' and a 'roof'. It's called a 'room'. I suggest the both of you ask around and find one before you lecture the whole country about being 'repressed'. If you don't like that idea, I suggest you move somewhere else. Try pulling this stunt in Pakistan. Take dear MP sir with you as well. Have fun getting stoned.*

I kept scrolling.

An NRI doctor living in Scotland commented: *How else do you expect these poor parents to react? Both the guy and the girl should get another tight slap now for airing their dirty laundry along with the dirty video. They should also file obscenity charges against this 'band'. Truly pathetic attempt. The song is bad too, by the way ...*

Some people continued defending Sree and Anita, saying the point wasn't *how* it happened, but everything that it *led to*. Didn't matter. Most were trying to get their jokes in and treating the whole affair as a free-for-all. The comments against Sree and Anita kept flowing.

Rishi knocked on the bathroom door. 'Everything okay?'

I'd been in there forty minutes and flushed six times.

'All good.'

'Any chance you might be getting out soon?'

That was also when I found out that Sree and Anita were in Bangalore. The article didn't mention it, but when I checked my Facebook inbox, one of the many people I'd messaged the previous night had replied with: *Nice you're here. I ran into your bro recently. You staying at his?*

I tried to push this new knowledge to the back of my skull so it could remain a rounded whole. But I felt I was now trespassing. That I ought to grab my bag, book another bus, and find a different city right away.

My chest started aching shortly after I flushed a seventh time and stepped out of the bathroom. I remembered Appa's Californian heart attack.

It got worse when Rishi's family came over to see him. Father, mother, sister. They'd brought lunch. These were the people you would never see on *Jeremy Kyle*.

Rishi's father did something with plane routes and cargo. He was wearing a white polo shirt that was stretched by his paunch. He called Rishi 'Rish'. Gave him a big slap on the back. His mother, tall and thin, was in a blue saree. She worked for the HR department of a baby-foods company. Rishi's sister was a college student. Her shirt told me to visit a surf shop in Honolulu.

All through lunch, while they laughed and talked, one part of me was thinking about the article, Appa and Amma back home, and Sree in Bangalore. The other part was trying to calculate if Rishi's family knew he was gay. I thought that if these people didn't know it, I'd feel much better. They mentioned Shashank a lot but this could have been because he was the roommate.

Rishi's sister teased, 'When's your shadow getting here?'

Rishi's parents discussed, at length, the pros and cons of some exam that Shashank was supposed to sit.

All inconclusive.

I gave up and tried to be social by asking everyone questions. Then I picked at my food. Each bite became a soggy clump.

After lunch, Rishi's family stayed for another three or four hours during which I listened to their advice about cracking the MBA exams. Shashank came in just as they were leaving. Briefly, they all huddled by the door. Rishi's mother said, 'Next time you won't escape us.'

I never did find out if Rishi's parents knew. It seemed like a clichéd thing to ask him: 'Do your parents know?' I was worried he might even say, 'Why does it matter? Are we in middle school?'

My chest and stomach were getting tighter. It felt like I'd swallowed lumps of clay.

'If you were already feeling so fucking shitty and on the verge of a fucking panic attack, why the fuck did you take edibles, you fucking moron?'

The slightly longer answer is this:

After Rishi's parents left, Shashank suggested that, it being Saturday and also my first evening in Bangalore, we ought to do something fun. Then he went to the kitchen and came back with a jar of gummies. Rishi, sensing something bad perhaps, said to me, 'We should postpone till tomorrow. You should probably just get some sleep tonight.'

But I was already too enthusiastic. I wanted to enter my morning state of mind. I guess I also thought I was feeling better.

At first, it really did go okay. Rishi put on some music and turned on his PS4. The lights were dimmed. Soft city sounds were coming in from the balcony.

Then while Shashank played an F1 game, Rishi opened a box of sweets that his mother had brought. Mysore Pak. A different kind from the ones you get in Trivandrum. I had two and then five, then ten. Somewhere along the way, it occurred to me that they were too waxy. Next thing I knew, it was coating the inside of my throat. There may be some metaphorical import to the trigger here, but the feeling was very real and very urgent.

Of course, reaching back there with your tongue is impossible. That didn't stop me from trying and gagging non-stop. The ghee smell started hurting my eyes and it wouldn't leave my hands no matter how many times I scrubbed them on my jeans. It started to mingle with my sweat. I felt the waxiness spreading and was convinced my throat was closing up. I couldn't breathe. A bag in my stomach rolled up and turned hard. I shivered and said, 'I don't feel good. I feel like I'm dying.'

From there, the intensity only increased. I suggested that they drive me to a hospital or call an ambulance. I screamed at them to take me seriously. Rishi said, 'Calm down and breathe through your nose. This is just a bad trip on pot and you have smoked pot plenty. All you need to do is sleep it off.'

Meanwhile, I had infected Shashank. He was walking around saying, 'Is he going to stop freaking out?'

When they moved to the shadows to talk, I wondered if they were discussing the fact that they had accidentally given me a wrong dose or the wrong drug entirely. I curled up on the floor, clutched my chest and, blubbering, waited for my life in review. Here I saw Appa, shaking open the morning paper: TRIVANDRUM YOUTH DIES OF DRUGS; NAKED BODY FOUND IN DITCH.

'Why was he naked?' Appa asks Amma.

Apparently it was somehow decided then that we would call Joel and he would call my brother. Joel caved as soon as Rishi introduced himself and explained the situation.

I say 'apparently', 'somehow', 'decided' but it was my idea really, despite my initial urge to run further from Sree's presence. Not thinking clearly and seeing death were definitely factors; I don't think it would have happened without the edibles. But another factor was that all evening I'd felt completely lost. I didn't want to return home and I didn't belong with these people. I suppose I wanted an evacuation.

I was blinking in and out of sleep when the door banged open. Sreenath was in the apartment swearing at everyone, especially me. From the floor, he seemed powerful like Godzilla. Sree was wearing a large hoodie and an old pair of jeans. He had vagabond hair and a dotty stubble.

To Rishi he said, 'Do I have a siren on my head? Do I look like an ambulance?' By then you could hear the neighbours stirring and Rishi just wanted me out of the house. Shashank had retreated to a corner. He was paranoid the police would show up.

Sree called an Uber. In the car, he said, 'I have a ton of crap to deal with as it is and you go and stage this? Fuck you.' He kept repeating it so much that the driver started complaining in Kannada.

The magnanimity I'd assigned to Sree disappeared. I wanted to say, 'How dare *you* act inconvenienced.' But there was a lot of traffic in my mouth. Puke, bile and just about every enzyme were queuing to make a break.

33

Maybe because of the drugs, the lack of sleep, a heavy migraine, and no electrolytes, the brief time I spent at Sree's place is all hazy vignettes.

At one in the morning, I woke up on a grey sofa in what turned out to be a two-bedroom apartment. A man wearing a skullcap was pacing between one of the inside rooms and the living room. He was reading an exam guide. Seeing me sit up, he knocked on the door of the second room and said, 'Your friend is awake.' Sree didn't come out. There were two missed calls on my phone, both from home. I fell back on the sofa and dozed off again.

At around three, I got up to find the bathroom and vomit. Now Sreenath was sitting at a small table in the corridor that ran alongside the inside rooms. He seemed to be reading comments on Facebook but switched tabs when he saw me.

The door of his room was half-open. Anita was on the bed scrolling her phone. Her hair was bobbed. She looked up and said, 'Oh lord, it's the marriage-maker. I wonder who the next lucky couple are', before closing the door.

I stood next to Sree for a while, feeling awkward – among other things, about the awkwardness I was feeling. I said, 'I didn't plan this, you know. I just happened to be in Bangalore. I wanted to get away from everything happening at home. I didn't even know you were here till a few hours back.'

'Sure.'

'*Sure*. You know you screwed up everyone's life, yes? *Sure*.'

Sree kept quiet. Now he was reading the front page of some blog.

I decided not to say anything more about the music video and asked him if he was okay.

'Don't start with that shit.'

'I get it if you don't want to come home.'

'Great.'

Sree's laptop screen was cracked at the edge. He himself looked somewhat unhealthy. His face had excess skin and it hung loose. His nails had a yellow tint.

I said, 'What was I supposed to do? Team up with you and what? I tried to find a way at least.'

To my surprise, Sree engaged. 'You always enabled them.'

'I tolerated them sometimes and tried to understand.'

'They sure returned the favour.'

'Even they were in a bind.'

'Okay.'

'But I do get your point.'

Sree shook his head, started saying something, stopped, then said it anyway: 'Even with that engineering shit, you were in my room every day asking me to just give in and do what they wanted. Every day you were in my room with your fucking appeals to reason.'

'I'm sorry,' I said. 'I was thirteen or fourteen.'

I really was. Sorry. And also thirteen or fourteen.

'You certainly didn't act that way. You acted like you were this old sage who knew everything inside out.'

'Somebody had to manage,' I said. 'Every time the house fell apart, every time Appa and Amma fought, every time we had an actual problem, you were aloof and useless.'

'Firstly, most of these problems, Appa and Amma created for themselves. It's what you get when you're vain and try to win the

187

approval of every single person. It's what you get when you're never satisfied or happy.'

Just so it was out there, I said, 'Everything we have, including our education, we have because of them.'

Sree only kept scrolling.

I sighed and told him I needed to go throw up.

'After talking to you, so do I.'

Because of the odd hour and my sudden displacement, it felt like our conversation had happened in a bubble.

When I got back from the bathroom, Sree was wearing head-phones. It was a blue pair and the fact that I'd never seen them before made me sad. I went back to the living room. Sree didn't ask me more about the Bangalore trip, how long I'd been there or if Appa and Amma were okay.

Whenever I opened my eyes, I saw the glow of his laptop and the edge of his body hunched on the stool. Early in the morning I heard him talking on the phone to someone I guessed was a lawyer.

The apartment was empty when I woke up. I washed my face, took a painkiller, and stood by Sree and Anita's door. It wasn't shut. Finally, I stepped inside.

The room was minuscule and tidy. The bed had floral sheets. Stephen King's *Mr. Mercedes* lay on the pillow. A skirt was draped for drying on the headboard. Pasted to the almirah door were Anita's sketches. In a few of them, Sree had drawn speech bubbles above the characters and written questions: 'Lunch?', 'Park?', 'Movie?'

I took the Stephen King book, tore the last couple of pages and put them in my pocket. Then feeling calmer, I pulled up a plastic chair and sat by the open window. The apartment was on the third floor. I could hear cycle bells and people chatting. I thought we might be near a university. The air smelled like talcum powder and detergent, along with a familiar Sree smell, the smell of our house.

By then, I'd already come to regret reaching out, in a manner, to him. It turned the Bangalore trip into a failure. But being in that room – the apparent cosiness, and what felt like the essence of a new family, forming – it made me linger and hope for some kind of reconciliation. Snow outside the window and all that.

Shortly before noon, Sree and Anita returned to the apartment followed by two girls. They turned out to be first-years writing for a university paper.

I had gone back to lying on the sofa. The girls interviewed Sree and Anita by the corridor table. I listened on and off, trying not to get angry and thinking of what I might say to Sreenath afterwards.

When the interview was over and Sree was showing the girls to the door, he stopped at the sofa and pointed to me. He said, 'This is what I was talking about earlier. What we have here is a typical Indian specimen called the "middleman".'

All three of them were grinning. I looked up as if from an operating table.

Sree, in a lecturer's voice, said, 'The middleman always finds a way to get to you, no matter how far you go. You can't hide from him. He doesn't have a spine and he doesn't like others having a spine. But he's always around to solve problems and help the world find peace. He's a shill.' Sree paused here to see if the girls would like to titter. 'Currently he's here from home on official shill business. It's like having a poltergeist that follows you house to house, except infinitely more annoying. You guys got that?'

I jumped up from the sofa and punched Sree in the face. Both of us fell on the floor. He pulled my hair and actually got a tuft of it in his hands. I spat on him and continued punching wherever I could. I made contact with teeth, then air, then an anonymous lump of flesh. The girls screamed.

Anita ran into the room and, in the same stride, kicked me hard on my nose.

The pain went everywhere like marbles and there were spots of blood all over my shirt. I crawled backwards until I felt the sofa. 'Fuck you,' I shouted. Or rather, 'Muck ew.'

Then I grabbed my phone and bag and wobbled towards the door.

Outside, I realised I didn't even know where I was. The spinning didn't help, nor did the blurry signs.

I jumped into the first idling auto and asked the guy to take me to the Madiwala bus stand. The blood seemed to scare him but he started the meter.

In the auto, I couldn't help but picture the journey back to Trivandrum. The exact reverse of my journey here. Boarding the bus full of sad people, having no music to listen to, going in the opposite direction of those joggers, standing at that rest stop with the wild grass, the urinary air, the moths. Finally reaching Thampanoor, taking an auto, going down that crater into Blue Hills.

When I saw the house in my head, I asked the driver to stop. I considered going to Rishi's apartment but was too embarrassed to do so right then. I googled cheap motels and gave the driver directions to what seemed like the closest one. Then I pulled out a sock from my bag, touched my nose to see if it was broken, and carefully wiped my face.

34

For the next two or three weeks it felt like an electrician was checking all the switches of my emotional circuit in a vengeful and surprising order. All of the extreme feelings were working great. I felt embarrassed, indignant, lost, loathsome, angry – and I felt so much and so fully that I also felt I was very important.

By the time I returned all those calls from Appa and Amma, they had decided they didn't want to talk to me unless I went back right away.

I thought:

Surely it's better to go home and return to the city later, with proper plans and money, than put my body on a motel bed in Paradise Inn that must be the most happening place for STDs.

And: Do I really want to risk the possibility of getting stabbed by the meth-powered bellman and that screwdriver in his pocket?

Do I want to become a ghost and haunt Room 114 for the rest of eternity?

Surely going home must be better than calling people I hadn't talked to since school or following up on those Facebook messages, and saying, *Hey, so I was wondering if I could crash with you for* –

Than listening to Nithin Krishnan brag about his fancy title, his tech money and his influencer girlfriend, or tolerating Manav Verma's yippie Pomeranian, or listening to Rishi again, complaining about how their neighbours had called the society president – all the while applying for jobs that didn't interest me one bit.

I thought, Surely packing it in is better than explaining our home situation over and over again to a dozen busybodies.

Or being centigrades away from an outburst all the time.

But I knew that if I went home it might take me years, perhaps, to gather the energy I needed to make another break.

35

The week I got a job – at DigiOn: Social media marketing, SEO, Content Creation, Strategy & Branding – was around the same time my parents gave in. It was towards the end of my second month in Bangalore. I'd just moved into a paying guest room. After Blue Hills, Elite Apartments and Paradise Inn, I was glad that this building was only called 'New PG Accommodations'. Of course it wasn't new; that goes without saying.

At New PG, my room was windowless and low-ceilinged, and the bathroom was a shared one at the far end of a narrow corridor. You only had to follow the smell. There were three floors and mine was the second one. The manager lived downstairs. His wife fried salmon every morning. You could reach their room by following the smell too.

On the day Amma finally called, she asked me if I needed anything and I said no. The next day, Appa called demanding to know where the hell the green scissors were.

For a while I tried to remain completely uninterested and stoic about the state of affairs at home. But once my parents started talking, I couldn't shut them up. I suppose I was concerned too.

In the months preceding the music video and its viral press, Appa and Amma had found some sort of a plateau – maybe it wasn't even a plateau, maybe it was a ledge. Whatever it was, it had seemed enough. Their interactions with neighbours had become more bearable. They had begun stepping out. Even our relatives had started getting used to us.

Naturally, it wasn't like anyone had moved on; there were still rumours flying about, and there were still plenty of people who were very awkward. But the point was, routine interactions had *started* happening again.

I guess it's one thing to suffer airborne rumours and another thing to have them published in newspapers. I also learned that while I was away, a local news crew, with the dish van and lights, had showed up at Blue Hills. They hadn't been allowed inside and nothing was filmed, but the channel had nonetheless aired a small segment about the music video later that same night.

To most residents of our colony, thirty seconds on an actual TV meant infinitely more than a trillion clicks online.

Amma complained that Karthika aunty was avoiding her. Appa rambled about how he would sue Sree for libel.

I'd googled him in those first few weeks. There were no further articles or interviews, though there was an op-ed about child porn, the ineffectiveness of site bans and the need for holding porn sites accountable. It mentioned the music video in passing.

Later, I realised that Sree and Anita, worried about obscenity charges, had by then removed the official version.

36

For a long time after that, things continued to sound bad at home. Appa and Amma kept trying to make me return. They did this for almost three months. During this period, I would get calls from Amma every other hour. She'd call whenever she'd had a disagreement with Appa. She'd call every time she thought somebody was being rude to her or she felt like crying or was worried about the future. Sometimes she'd call and ask me to stay on the phone while she shopped at the supermarket or went to the ATM.

I thought my parents would try and sell their house and leave Blue Hills, but they haven't yet. Anita's mother, I heard, had left Trivandrum for her husband's native place in Kollam.

It's May now. These days Appa and Amma call less and less. I wouldn't say things have become better, but they haven't exactly become worse.

Appa keeps talking about buying another car – at the moment, it's a third-hand Benz. No way he can afford that.

Sometimes he talks about expanding the business. Amma, too, has started working at the shop on an almost full-time basis. She told me it felt more appropriate than being a teacher.

*

A few weeks back, something else happened at Blue Hills. Salil, the 25-year-old guy with the Duke bike and the bad rep, was arrested for dealing marijuana. The police had detained him for three days before dropping him home in a jeep, sirens blazing.

'That's all everyone is talking about now,' Amma said. She seemed annoyed.

Once in a rare while, she asks about Sreenath. Until recently, I kept thinking I might run into him. Then Joel told me he had actually moved to Bombay a long time back. Anita too. He works in the finance department of an advertising firm. She does something similar. According to Joel, they haven't had much contact with anyone.

37

I still work at the same marketing firm. Most people here are aware of my relationship to the video because I mentioned it to them. Not saying anything, as I got to know them more and more, felt like a lie by omission, especially since many knew of the incident itself. I suppose I also wanted to get it out of the way, a full disclosure.

Three weeks back, a colleague of mine, a photographer, told me that he had this idea of making a documentary about the video fiasco from start to finish. We were sitting in front of his computer, waiting for it to throw up a giant Photoshop file.

'You could direct it,' he said. 'And have full editorial discretion and all that jazz. Remember the documentary about student suicides at IIT? This could be like that. The scope, that is. Three hundred and sixty degrees. And all that jazz.'

The colleague – his name is Bipin – is one of those people who is very curious about the video. He went through a similar phase at home when his sister got pregnant.

'It was a blockbuster,' he said.

We both got excited talking about it – the documentary, not his sister's pregnancy – and afterwards it attached itself to my brain.

I thought about the idea so much that I mentioned it to Trisha, my old college friend, when we hung out.

Trisha had gone to Bombay for her internship, but England hadn't taken her in.

'I can't believe I had a fucking farewell party,' she keeps saying.

She of course knew about the video already.

Trisha now works for a Bangalore paper. Her office building is next to mine and, because she got rid of her paranoid boyfriend, we often talk. I have mixed feelings about how well-adjusted she is.

Anyway, when we met up last week, we talked about the documentary. We were on the terrace of her apartment, drinking some Scotch that this Kashmiri guy she met on Bumble had left before he flew off.

'That's the stupidest thing I have ever heard,' she said. 'Let sleeping dogs die. And I do mean die.'

I told her that the documentary wouldn't really be a documentary. It would just be a short piece that sets everything straight and shows everybody in a clearer light and gives everybody peace of mind. It would be like an epitaph of the incident. Closure, so to speak. I could talk to all those involved, even Anita's mother and father. I could get them to describe the circumstances, the confusion. I could also have them talk about how they feel now. It would be our way to reclaim the story and then move on.

'You'll just make it worse,' Trisha said. We were watching a plane blink across the sky. 'When you get a pimple, you should just leave it alone, no matter how much you want to touch it.'

I told her that I knew Sree's music-video stunt was about 'taking control of the narrative' and that, yes, it had only exacerbated the problem. But with the right fittings this could be different.

Trisha said, 'Your life, buddy.'

Last Sunday, I considered calling Joel for Sreenath's number.

When I thought about Sree, what I remembered was the way he had talked to those college girls, the journalists. They had looked like they didn't want to be there in the first place. Sree babbled a lot: about his plans to become some kind of a producer, about how they were smart to leverage their situation the way they did, about philosophy and politics, most of which didn't even make sense. He cracked a lot of bad jokes too.

One of the girls had casually asked, 'So whose idea was it anyway? Going to that place in the video?'

Sree said, 'Just happened.'

Anita said, 'His.'

The girls laughed nervously.

After a few seconds of silence, Anita said, 'Fine: forty me, sixty you. Cool, Sree?'

Sree didn't say anything.

Lying in bed, I remembered this and I remembered all the blame-accounting that Appa and Amma used to do. The fifteen per cents and the ten per cents and even the three per cents that were fought over and tabulated. I wondered if Sree and Anita might be different. I thought again about how the documentary might help clarify some of these equations and maybe even balance a few books.

Then, just as I was seriously considering my call to Joel, I got a text about some urgent work that needed to be sent out. And while I was doing that, the carpenter finally arrived to fix my cupboard lock. By the time he left, I had to go see a friend about an old bike. I also had to visit my landlord for a reimbursement, repair my laptop charger, return some books, and get groceries.

By evening I was tired, then somehow happy about the tiredness, and then guilty about the happiness. I went for a walk in one of the quieter lanes near my building and languidly smoked a cigarette like in the movies. In my head, I made a long list of things I had to do over the coming days. I wanted to believe Sree had a long list too. Maybe, as we both went about what Appa calls 'the hassles of life', surviving and crossing things off, we'd one day find ourselves face to face. Maybe he'll call me a moron or maybe I'll punch him or maybe he'll say *help* or maybe we'll both decide to keep walking. Maybe all of us will add one another on Facebook and act like friends.

Acknowledgements

Many thanks to:

Luke Brown, my genius editor, for seeing the best in this book; Sarah-Jane Forder for her wisdom and patience; Hannah Westland, Graeme Hall, Flora Willis, Anna-Marie Fitzgerald, and everyone at Serpent's Tail

My incredible agent Ivan Mulcahy and whatever he eats for breakfast. Without him this book wouldn't exist. And everyone at MMB Creative

Samar Hammam at Rocking Chair Books for helping this go places I couldn't have imagined

Jonathan Myerson, Clare Allan and Anthony Cartwright, amazing teachers

My mother Seetha Jayakumar for her brilliance and inspiration; my father Jayakumar for all his support; my hilarious sister Nandana Jayan; my cool brother Ananth L; my grandfather Thanu Pillai

Ushnav Shroff for hanging around

Maria Chirayil for perpetual reassurances

Sarita Vellani at Toto Funds the Arts, Michelle D'costa, Tanuj Solanki, Megha Agarwal and Krittika Basu for early help with writing

Nanditha Kalidoss, Sandeep Rajguru, Nina Eidem, Simon Lörsch, Faiza Khan, Saurabh KV Kamalakaran, Dilin Mathew, Vaishakh Kolaprath, Naveen Fernando, Savio Victor, Lakshmy Venkatesh